A FAMILIAR BETRAYAL

BRIANNA NORTH

Also by Brianna North:
Stay Strong
The Other Half of Me
Where the Sun Won't Shine

Copyright © 2024 Brianna North

All rights reserved. This book or any portion thereof may not be reproduced or used in any manner whatsoever without the express written permission of the publisher except for the use of brief quotations in a book review.

Book design by Brianna North
Cover design by Brianna North
Cover image by Eberhard Grossgasteiger
Pexels.com

This is a work of fiction. Names, characters, places, and incidents are either the product of the author's imagination or are used fictitiously, and any resemblance to actual persons living or dead, business establishments, events, or locales is entirely coincidental. Cover models used for illustrative purposes only and may not endorse or represent the book's subject

To my friends and family, who remain my biggest supporters and first readers.

To my readers, who are the reason I write. Without you, these books would never exist.

PROLOGUE

I was ten years old the first time I tried to run.

We were in the Walmart parking lot, of all places. Mommy had just wrapped up filming our grocery trip for the vlog—apparently, internet strangers needed to know *everything* we ate—and Daddy's hand gripped my shoulder with alarming force. "Alyssa, stop dragging your feet on the ground," he growled in my ear. "Don't you know how to do anything right?"

In Daddy's eyes, I was always failing, from the way I learned at school to the way I ate my cereal in the morning. Nothing could shield me from his constant criticism. And that day, right there in the parking lot, I decided I'd had enough. So I started running.

Over the rushing wind in my ears, I heard Mommy release a shriek of surprise. Her heavily pregnant body wouldn't allow her to come after me, so Daddy's footsteps followed me instead. "Alyssa!" His booming voice sent an electric wave of fear through my body. "Where do you think you're going? What's wrong with you?"

It dawned on me, then, that I might've made a *big* mistake. If—when—Daddy caught me, I'd be in for the worst punishment of my life. I didn't even know where I was going. But still, I pumped my legs harder.

People loading their groceries in their cars watched me zip by. I wanted them to hear my thoughts, to know how desperately I needed to get away. The thing about Daddy was that he wasn't always like this, and sometimes I loved him with every fibre of my being. But when these bad moods overcame him, his anger was unpredictable. Today, I decided I couldn't stand it a second longer; I needed a new family, one that said nice things to me, one that didn't shove a camera in my face every waking second. There were tons of families in this parking lot, and they were probably a thousand times better than mine. Maybe they could adopt me.

Daddy's strong hand suddenly clamped down on my arm, and he tugged me backward with such force that I toppled over, scraping my knee on the concrete. "Get in the car," he hissed.

My taste of freedom was over just as quickly as it'd started. I screamed. He shushed me as people started to stare, and before I knew it, he was shoving me in the back of the car. Mommy and my little sister Harper were already buckled in and waiting. "Honey, why would you do that?" Mommy asked, turning the vlog camera toward me.

I wanted to break the stupid thing. I said nothing.

"Do you have anything to say for yourself? You scared Mommy really badly."

"Just leave me alone!" I snapped.

She angled the camera so that it was facing herself. "So it looks like Miss Alyssa is having a really tough day," she told our viewers. "She's gotten to the age where she likes to test our patience, and she needs to know that's not okay. When we get home, she's definitely getting sent to her room and gets no TV for a week. If you're a parent of a child around this age, comment down below what your experience has been when it comes to attitude and how you deal with it. I'd love to know."

My face burned hot with rage. I was totally going to look like the biggest brat ever in this vlog, and everyone at school would tell me so. I crossed my arms and stared out the window as Daddy ducked into the car. He didn't address me; he waited until Mommy stopped vlogging before telling her, "There's something seriously wrong with that kid. What did we do wrong?"

The tears came hot and fast. There was nothing worse than the feeling that your parents hated you.

CHAPTER 1

Six years later, not much has changed except for one thing: I barely see Dad anymore.

Mom and Dad divorced last year, and Dad left town, only reaching out every once in a while to check on my siblings and I. He refuses to speak to Mom; he says she ruined his life. She says he ruined hers. Dad's still occasionally filled with all-encompassing rage. Mom's still obsessed with the internet's opinion on our family. Clearly they were *not* meant for each other.

What can I say; ten-year-old me would be pissed to know that things are still pretty much the same as they were back then.

Today, Mom has me positioned in the backyard against the lilac tree as she snaps photos of me for our latest clothing brand sponsorship. I desperately need to study for my chemistry final on Monday, but work for the vlog always comes first. The floral crop top is itchy against my skin, and the baggy mom jeans are so baggy, in fact, that they hardly stay on my body. "Smile with your teeth," she directs as I jut my hips out in a ridiculous pose. "And face me a little more. You're too sideways."

Sometimes, I like doing sponsorships. I mean, I like free clothes just as much as anyone, especially if they can give me some sort of confidence boost. Taking gorgeous photos can make me feel like a whole different person. But today is not one of those days. Today, I'd rather swim in lava than take *another* round of photos to please Mom's subscribers and this brand's marketing team.

"Alyssa, you're fake-smiling again." Mom blows out a frustrated breath. "I can tell. Everyone will be able to tell. I need a *real* smile. Can you just cooperate for five minutes?"

I'd give you a real smile if you'd put the fucking camera away. "I am."

"No, you're not. The ad is supposed to go up by the end of the day today, and I'll need these photos done within the hour so I can edit them in time. You're not making this easy."

"You're the one nitpicking."

Her eyes narrow, and my *real smile* finally makes a brief appearance. "Watch your tone."

One of the things I hear the most at school is that it "must be nice" to be internet famous. It "must be nice" that so many people love me and want to be like me and want to have the perfect family. Truth is, we are, in fact, the furthest thing from perfect. Don't let the stunning house, expensive car, luxury vacations and 4.3 million subscribers fool you; Mom only films what she wants you to see, just like every other vlog channel. She's also the reason I don't have friends.

My classmates only watch our vlogs to find things to tease me for. They've watched a twenty-minute video entirely dedicated to my first period, all of which included shopping for pads, showing me how to put one on, and a humiliating explanation of how having my period means I'm becoming a woman. They've watched me throw tantrums, puke, have accidents, and more recently, experience a sex talk from Mom because a boy dared to talk to me at a resort we were staying at. There are no limits to the kind of content Mom makes, as long as we're making money.

The strangers who watch us probably think I'm the most popular girl in school, with hordes of girls my age just *dying* to be my friend. They couldn't be more wrong.

Robyn McNeill's mocking voice blasts through my eardrums whenever I think of school. "*Hey Bennett FamJams, it's Alyssa, and welcome back to our channel*!" she says in what's quite possibly the most annoying falsetto voice I've ever heard. She pretends to hold a vlog camera in front of her face. Very original. "*Today we're going to be talking about the time I shit my pants at Disneyland*!"

Now, Mom directs me to take one of the lilac branches in my hands and pretend to smell the flowers. I turn sideways, and just as my fingers swipe along the branch, Mom's grating voice fills my ears again. "Oh, honey, you're going to have to suck that tummy in. You haven't been working out lately, have you?"

Embarrassment climbs through my veins, and my face flushes. I fight the urge to crush the flowers in my hands. "No." I say nothing else and instead do as told, sucking my stomach in as far as I can to give the illusion that I didn't gain weight—AKA Mom's worst nightmare. Now she's going to make me work out every day until she sees some kind of improvement, and a heavy dread sets in my stomach at the thought. Why can't she just leave me alone for once?

It's another thirty minutes before she's satisfied with my little performance and lets me back into the house. I rush through the sliding patio doors before she can get the chance to ask me if I want to see the pictures. I can't get to my room fast enough.

Up in my room, I scroll through Instagram as I wait for Mom. Within an hour, she logs into my account and uploads the ad:

I am summer lovin' this cozy outfit from @BreezyBoutique! A new haul is coming to our channel tomorrow so you can see all my fav pieces. Use my code ALYSSABENNETT15 for 15% off your entire order! #BreezyBoutiquePartner #BreezyBeautiful #summerwardrobe

Only three of the nearly two hundred photos we took make the cut. It's a wonder I still have my sanity.

The praising comments roll in like a tidal wave, but I don't read them anymore; they've become as much a part of my daily routine as brushing my teeth. I'm still grateful for them, for how privileged I am to live this kind of life, and on days like today, I tend to forget that. I realize I've been scrolling this app for far too long, considering I have studying to do, so I finally put the phone down and open my chemistry book.

The word problems outlined in our study guide look like another language to me, but if I don't pass this final, I won't pass the class. Mom can't know this, but I'm nearly failing chemistry. It would destroy her dreams of getting me into an Ivy League college, and she might not ever forgive me; after all, what would our subscribers think if I didn't get into Stanford, especially since Mom has been mentioning it in our vlogs for years?

I can't stand to be a failure anymore. So I get to work.

Just as I scribble out the final calculation, my little sister Harper bursts through my bedroom door, cradling her rose gold iPhone in her hand. A twinge of annoyance travels through my gut. "What do you want?" I ask.

She holds the phone out to me. "Dad wants to talk to you."

My heart gallops. It's been almost a month since he last called, and honestly, I've started to miss him. Sometimes I think the distance has made our relationship stronger, but on days like today, I miss having his strong arms around me, hearing his laugh, living a normal life with two parents who get along. Things with Dad weren't horrible all the time. I try not to be bothered that he didn't call me directly as I take the phone from Harper's hand and press it to my ear. "Hey, Dad."

"Hey, Lissy. Just wanted to check in and see how things are going." His deep voice fills the speaker, sending a wave of calm over me.

I lean back in my chair and wave Harper away from my doorway. "I'm all right. Just have a couple finals coming up, then school's out."

"Well, that's exciting. Have any plans for the summer?"

"Probably. I know Mom's taking us to Niagara Falls tomorrow, but not sure what else she has planned."

Dad sighs. "Yeah, Harper told me. Have fun. I'm hoping to drop by for a visit next week if your mother doesn't plan any more spontaneous trips."

There's an edge to his voice, and guilt ripples through my chest. "I want to see you again. I just wish you and Mom would at least talk to each other every once in a while."

"Trust me, Lissy, I wish things were different. I'm trying. It's not easy, but I know it's really taking a toll on you guys. I'll get the courage to talk to her again one day."

Can that 'one day' be, like, next week when you visit? "You promise?"

He blows out a breath. "I promise. But like she said, she needs to move on, so I need to let her do that."

I nod along, even though he can't see me. Every time we talk, our conversation always steers toward Mom, followed by passive aggressive comments about how things didn't work out. It's exhausting, so I circle back to our earlier topic of school, which is somehow better. We go over the basics (my grades, classes I'm taking next year, etc.,) until we arrive at my least favourite talking point: college. "Still thinking about Stanford? Or what you want to major in?"

My stomach turns to jello. Stanford is just as much his dream for me as it is Mom's, so I choose my next words carefully. "Not really. It's just that…I don't know, Stanford is really far away. Like, in a totally different country, and—"

"You don't want to go." It's not a question. His tone sharpens slightly. "You can tell me the truth."

I gulp. "I…no, I don't, to be honest."

He sighs. "Okay. If that's what you want, that's fine. But why don't you want to go? Is it because of your mother? Did she say something to you?"

His words strike a nerve, and red creeps into the corners of my vision. His favourite pastime lately is to villainize her for everything, including things that have never happened. I can tell he's trying to hold his anger back, which somehow fuels my own. My hand squeezes tighter around the phone so I don't throw it across the room. "Not everything is about her! This is *my* decision about *my* future. I'm just thinking about me for once. And I don't want to go."

"Cut the attitude, Alyssa," he snaps, venom coating his words. "I'm just asking you why you don't want to go. You don't need to get all defensive."

"I want to stay closer to home. And I don't even know what I want to do."

"But you'll figure that out. You have a year. And we'd come to visit you all the—"

"I'm staying here."

He sighs audibly. "At least promise me you'll *go* to college. I don't want you thinking that you're going to make it in life as an influencer. You need to get a real job. That stupid vlog isn't going to last forever."

I'm so over this conversation. "I will."

He cuts the conversation short and asks to speak to Levi, my seven-year-old brother. I bring Harper's phone down the hall and open Levi's door to find him sprawled out on his floor, building a tower out of his Legos. "It's for you," I say as I hand him the phone, then bolt out of his room.

When I get back to my room, I throw myself down on my bed and yank the blankets over my face. Why can't our family be normal again?

CHAPTER 2

"Here we are, in Niagara Falls! And look at this view." Mom pivots the vlog camera away from her face toward the scenic lookout of the Falls below. It's a bright, cloudless morning, and the water sparkles in the sun. "I just can't get enough of this. Are you guys excited?"

Harper and Levi each give a loud cheer, but I just stare out at the Falls, silent. Unlike Mom, I'd rather live in the moment than take in the view through the lens of a camera. I should be grateful to be here, but today is one of those days where I'd rather be curled up in my bed reading a book.

"Alyssa, you didn't say anything. What about you?"

I give a quick shrug. "Yeah, I'm excited."

"Good to hear!" Then she's back to telling our audience all about the fun things there are to do here, from the SkyWheel to MarineLand to Niagara Speedway go-karting. My siblings and I wait not-so-patiently for her to finish; my feet are itching to get moving, and Harper has already started down the sidewalk. I fight the urge to tell Mom that if our viewers really want to visit Niagara Falls, one simple Google search will tell them about all the attractions.

As Mom continues, some of the other tourists begin to stare. Instinctually, I turn away, wishing I could shrivel up and disappear. My cheeks heat with embarrassment. No matter how many times this happens when we're in public—and it happens *a lot*—I'll never get used to the judgment coating their expressions, especially from the older generations. More than once, I've heard them grumble about how *back in their day*, there wasn't a cellphone in sight, that they didn't have photo evidence of everything they did in one day. Sometimes I wish we could go back to those days.

"Mom, I thought we were going to get funnel cakes?" Harper stops walking and throws up her hands.

"In a minute." Mom has put away the camera, and now she barely glances up from her phone to acknowledge my sister. "We're going to take some photos first."

We all let out a collective groan. A fire lights inside my stomach. "Can't we just do that after?" I practically beg. "I don't feel like being in photos right now."

"Just a few. It won't take long."

"Please, Mom? I look like shit right now."

"You look fine, Alyssa. Come here."

Reluctantly, I heavily drag my feet over to where she's standing, closer to the lookout. Mom isn't the kind of person to give up easily. She pulls us all in for a few selfies first before positioning her camera on our tripod, and I make sure I have my widest, brightest smile on proud display. It's hot as hell out here; my striped shirt sticks to my body, and a thick coat of sweat has formed on my forehead. Not the best look for photos, but Mom will Facetune the results to her liking.

"Are we going to get funnel cakes now?" Harper asks as we wrap up the photoshoot. She bounces on her toes like an impatient toddler. "We were supposed to, like, twenty minutes ago."

My stomach rumbles; funnel cakes wouldn't be such a bad idea. "I agree. I'm starving."

"Me three!" Levi pipes up.

Mom shakes her head as she scrolls through the photos on her phone. Her shoulders are slumped. "Just a few more, then we can go. These photos didn't really turn out; you can barely see the Falls in the back."

I don't know whether it's the heat getting to me or the fact that this scene is so familiar to me, but the anger boiling in my stomach finally erupts out of my mouth. "Who cares? It's not like everyone won't know we're in Niagara Falls. Can we just have a normal day? *Please*?"

"Watch your tone," she warns. "I'm not asking for much. And what's that supposed to mean; '*a normal day*?'"

A lump lodges itself in my throat, killing the words I want to say. Do I dare try and tell her how I really feel? Will she accuse me of ruining the trip? With Mom, you never know what the outcome will be. But as I look to my siblings, I know they feel the same, and it's about time someone spoke up.

I suck in a deep breath and finally say, "I'm just sick of pretending like we're so perfect."

Mom rears back, and her nostrils flare. "We're not pretending anything, Alyssa. Is that all you think this is? So we take a trip, and I'm not allowed to take a single family photo?"

"*Mom*, let's go," Harper whines.

"I'm not finished." Mom doesn't look at Harper; just keeps her gaze trained on me. "If people watching our vlogs think we're perfect, then that's their problem. But maybe you're right. Maybe we need to stop sharing only the good moments on our channel. Would it make you feel better if we talked more about the bad moments, too?"

Bad moments. We definitely have those, but is it really our viewers' business? "I don't know." I drop down onto a nearby bench and wipe the sweat from my forehead. Gross. "We don't have to share everything."

"Then I don't understand what you want. You don't want us to only share good moments, but you don't want us to share any bad moments either?"

She's backed me into a corner; she's sort of right. I don't really know what I want, and besides, even if I tell her what I want, she'll just tell me it's her channel. *Her* channel, until she needs my siblings and I to make her some money.

That's a conversation for another day; I won't go there.

"You do have a point, though," Mom continues. She motions for me to move over so she can sit. "It'll make us more authentic. People don't relate to influencers if they don't seem like they have any struggles. And we have struggles; take, for instance, the situation with your father and I." She pauses for a moment to yell at Harper and Levi to stop wandering away. "No one knows the full story. What if we tell them what happened?"

My stomach clenches. "That's just going to make him mad."

She scoffs and waves her hand. "Oh, he won't see the video."

She really has no idea how obsessed he is with hating her. "Are you sure about that?"

"I'm positive, Alyssa. He doesn't watch the channel. The channel is the biggest reason we're not together anymore."

She couldn't be more accurate, which soothes my nerves a little. My mind wanders back to all the explosive fights of last year; Mom slamming doors and screaming that she's the family breadwinner, Dad arguing back that he can't even take a shit without the internet knowing. Mom exclaiming that she can't stop the vlog, that it's her passion, Dad retorting with something along the lines of, "It's creepy how obsessed people are with us. That's not normal." Fat chance in hell he's ever watched a single vlog since he moved out; I'm sure our videos raise his blood pressure.

A part of me is still hesitant to let Mom tell that story. "Even if he doesn't watch the video himself, what if someone tells him about it?"

Mom tugs at the fabric of her "I Love Niagara Falls" t-shirt. The heat is finally getting to her, I see. "Let them. What is he going to do about it, anyway?"

"*Moooom.*" Harper stomps her foot.

"Harper, cut it out!" Mom's raised voice pierces the air. "Give me a minute."

"I gave you a minute ten minutes ago!"

Mom sighs heavily just as a family approaches us, their cellphones raised. I know they're about to ask to take a photo with us. "We'll continue this conversation later," she tells me. "But we'll start filming tomorrow. Sound good to you?"

Not really, but whatever. "Sure."

NEW VIDEO FROM THEBENNETTFAM
*FINALLY TALKING ABOUT THE DIVORCE *EMOTIONAL**

 Hey Bennett FamJams, it's Melissa, and welcome back to our channel. Today's video is going to be a lot different from the videos we usually post, and it's been something that, to be honest, I've been dreading talking about. And that's not like me; I've always been someone who's not shy to share the good and bad about my life, but for some reason...I don't know, it felt like I could never find the right time to tell my story. But I think it could help a lot of people out there who may be going through the same thing.

 If you've been following us for a long time, you know that Dan and I divorced a while back, which was probably a bit of a shock to you guys since he was such a big part of this channel and its growth. We announced it, and then just kind of...left it at that. You guys didn't get any sort of explanation, and I didn't really think it was necessary. Until now. I think it's easy for any influencer to show that their lives are perfect, and I'll admit that I fell into that trap, even though my relationship was so toxic.

 A lot of this stuff might be hard for you guys to hear, but what you see on social media isn't always real. You never truly know what's going on behind the scenes. I just want you to know that if you've experienced anything like this, you're not alone, and I sincerely hope you find a solution to your situation.

 So, to get into the story. When Dan and I had Alyssa, we were still in high school, and we married right after graduation. He was super supportive of my YouTube journey in the beginning because it kept me busy. He knew how lonely it was for me to be at home with a baby while he was in school and at work, and when he saw that I had started to make money from my hobby, he encouraged me to keep going. But because he's such a private person, he started to resent it.

That's where most of our marital problems started to happen. He would criticize me every time I filmed, and for a long time, it made me incredibly insecure, until I realized I shouldn't have to be insecure about something I'm passionate about. It drove a wedge between us, to be honest, and our personalities just clashed. And when he started to take out his anger on the kids...God, I'm already getting emotional.

It was never physical; I will say that. But he'd just snap at the kids, which is when I started to have a problem. Yelling, calling them names...that sort of thing. I'm never okay with that. It's not their fault we had problems in our marriage, which I find myself reminding the kids time and time again. It will never be their fault.

I remember around Christmas a couple years ago, Harper was trying to put the star on the top of our tree, and it kept wobbling. He was holding her upright, and he got so fed up with her that he put her back on the floor and said, "All right, dumbass, guess I'll do it." She cried the rest of the night that Daddy was being mean and took a special moment away from her, and when I confronted him about it, he just told me I was crazy. He said I'm the reason the kids will grow up "soft." That I can't just let them do whatever they want. That they need to grow a thicker skin. It made me realize he was cutting them down in attempt to build them up. And that's not right.

I couldn't let that happen.

That's just one example out of the hundreds I probably have, but it got to a point where I had to tell myself the kids deserved better. I deserved better. And being in a toxic household wasn't good for them. So I asked for a divorce.

Dan wasn't on board with it at first, but when he finally left, he decided to drain our bank account. Yes, you heard that right; he took all the money that I earned to feed our kids, while our kids were under my roof. All because he didn't feel that I had a "real" job, that I didn't work hard. But he was happy to take all the money that came with it.

It was a very long battle to get the money back. I was hardly making any of our mortgage payments, and so I tried to shift back into daily vlogging to earn some extra money. I won't be the first to admit that trying to pretend like you're happy when you're not...that's not easy. Looking back at our videos from that time, you guys can probably tell they're not one hundred percent authentic, and I'm sorry for that.

At the end of the day, my top priority is making sure my kids are taken care of and are happy. Being a mother is a job that comes before YouTube, always. The situation was really taking a toll on them, and that hurt me more than anything, so I needed to take a step back. We took a break from YouTube, got our court dates scheduled, and now we're lucky if Dan sees the kids three times a year. But that's his choice.

It's a choice I wish could be different. But what can you do, right?

CHAPTER 3

The video hits a million views within the first 24 hours.

It's not the first time a video on TheBennettFam channel has seen this kind of success. Mom started out as a teen mom vlogger when I was born, and one of her first videos was a "Day in the Life of a Teen Mom at School," which reached one million views just as quickly. People became drawn to her because they saw her as a hardworking teenager who never gave up despite the obstacles she faced. So many of our viewers grew up with her—grew up with *us*—and they seemed to take the divorce personally.

And with the desire for drama, they've come back to our channel to watch Mom spill the beans about what happened.

Mom has really set the scene for a dramatic video; dark lighting, hardly any makeup, tissues conveniently placed on the bedside table for when she needs to dab at her wet eyes. It's more "authentic" that way, so people don't think she's trying too hard to be perfect in such a serious moment. She has it all down to a science.

As I watch the video in bed, I wonder where Dad is right now, what he's doing. If he's seen the video yet. Something in the back of my brain nags that he'll see this, that it'll piss him off, especially since the video is trending. Mom would say she has the right to tell her story, and technically, she isn't wrong. But there's a slight relief in the fact that it's not me he'll be mad at.

The video is twenty-four minutes long. Mom spends all of it bashing Dad in every way possible.

It's a bit of an eye-opener, though, because some of the incidents she's mentioned…I've never known about. When she gets to the part about Dad draining the bank account, I gasp and shrink under the covers. Did he really do that? Mom never showed any signs of struggling financially; maybe she was just really good at covering it up?

My blood starts to boil. The audacity Dad has.

Mom probably didn't tell me because she didn't want me to view Dad differently. But by uploading this video, it's pretty difficult not to. He *was* also mean to us; she's definitely not wrong about that. I think back to that time I tried to run away at Walmart—*"There's something seriously wrong with that kid"*—and my hands begin to shake. As the video continues, a part of me is glad he's not living here anymore, glad Mom made this video.

"Dan became a completely different person from the sweet guy I knew in high school," Mom says through the speakers of my laptop. "I gave up so much of my life to become a mom at a young age. It was my choice, and I was very aware of what came with it. Dan got to go off and make a career for himself, but it seemed like he never respected any of my sacrifices."

My parents had me when they were seventeen, and Mom never had the chance to build the career she wanted as a lawyer. While attending school full-time and working at a coffee shop part-time while she was pregnant, she discovered a mommy vlogging community on YouTube and decided to start making her own videos. They didn't blow up right away—not until I was about four months old—but once they did, she decided that this was what she was meant to do all along. Dad went to college to become a CPA while she stayed home making videos…and the rest is history.

With college on the horizon for me, it makes me wish I could experience something life-changing that would spell out my future career path in big bold letters. Right now, that part of my life is a huge question mark, and I don't have much time left to figure it out. Mind you, I don't need to get knocked up to reach this conclusion, but maybe I can do *something*, like travel the world, to open my eyes to all the possibilities out there. I'm not meant to be some member of a vlogging channel for the rest of my life.

God, I'm doing it again; wasting time on the internet when I should be studying, considering my chemistry final is tomorrow morning, but somehow that stresses me out more. Pick your poison, I guess.

Instead, I close my laptop and place it on my bedside table as I reach to turn off my lamp. My eyes burn with exhaustion; I'll probably watch the rest tomorrow. After I've done my exam, of course.

***

Moments after the soul-crushing chemistry exam, my phone lights up with a text. *Can you pick up Harper and Levi from school on your way home? Stopping at the store.*

Mom couldn't have picked a worse time. I fight the urge to roll my eyes and type, *Yeah sure.*

The drive home is only five minutes, but it feels like an hour. Harper and Levi drone on about how excited they are for summer break, and though I'd love to share their joy, I just want to sulk in my room alone. I probably failed the exam, and Mom is going to kill me. So is Dad, if I ever decide to tell him. I should've studied more last night instead of watching her stupid video.

"Alyssa, watch out!" Harper shouts, and my heart accelerates as I realize I've just blown a red light. A horn blares from somewhere behind me.

"Sorry," I say with a sheepish grin. "Had a bit of a bad day and can't concentrate, I guess."

"You're a bad driver. Sorry, not sorry."

I shrug off her comment and make a right into our driveway. I don't have the energy to defend myself, so I park and get out without another word. She's eleven, but sometimes I swear she's sixteen with that attitude.

Once in the house, I head straight to my room and pluck my current read off my bedside table: The Silent Patient by Alex Michaelides. There's something about reading that instantly soothes my tensed muscles and allows me to temporarily forget the world, even if 95% of my chosen books are thrillers. Admittedly, it comforts me to know that if I'm ever having a bad day, at least my life isn't nearly as bad as these characters' lives. I curl up underneath my blankets in bed and open the book to where I left off, losing myself in the rollercoaster of a story. I only have a few chapters left, so just like any other thriller, this is the point in the story where it starts to get intense, impossible to put down.

My phone buzzes next to me, and Mom's contact lights up the screen. *Ugh, what does she want now?* I scoop up the phone and press it to my ear. "Hello?"

"Hey, I forgot to mention something earlier," she says. Chatter explodes behind her; she's definitely still at the store. "We're going to film a thank-you video when I get home. Did you see that we reached 1.5 million views?"

Yep. "No, I didn't. That's cool."

"I know, right? How did the exam go?"

Dread travels through my core. "It was fine."

"Good to hear. I should be there in about twenty minutes, so start getting ready and tell Harper and Levi. We've gotten so much support in the comments, so I figured we'd film something to thank them."

For once, I'm glad she's steered the conversation toward the channel and not school. "Okay, sounds good. I'll let them know."

"Perfect. I'll see you soon." *Click.*

I look down at my ripped jean shorts and old t-shirt, and decide I don't need to change my outfit for the video. Instead, I untangle my dark hair from its ponytail; this is good enough. I'll tell Harper and Levi to get ready when I'm done this chapter.

I resume reading and am just about to finish the page when I hear the doorbell ring. "I'll get it!" Harper cries from downstairs, and I shake my head. Mom says we're not supposed to answer the door, especially when she's not home, and Harper knows that. Whatever, though; I'm tired of babysitting her. I shove the thought away and start the next chapter.

That's when I hear the ear-splitting scream.

I bolt upright in bed. "Harper?" I call out. Before I know it, I'm sprinting as fast as my legs will carry me to the stairs.

For a moment, I wondered if I've imagined the sound, if I've been reading too many thrillers lately, but the second scream turns my blood cold. Without looking, I already know my worst fear is coming true; someone—a crazed fan, maybe—is trying to get into the house. And they might hurt my little sister.

Not only that, but Mom isn't home to help us.

Levi's bedroom door bangs open, and suddenly he's hot on my heels. "Go back to your room and close the door," I demand.

"What's happening?" Tears slide down his cheeks.

"I don't know."

"Alyssa!" Harper's strangled voice is distant now.

I shove Levi down the hallway. "Go!"

The slam of his door echoes behind me, and I race down the stairs, stumbling on the last few. My eyes dart toward the front door in search of Harper, but I don't see her. The door is wide open. "Harper!" I yell again, desperation coating my voice. I have to find her. Someone must've taken her.

Before I get the chance to run, a firm hand clamps down on my shoulder. My heart jumps into my throat as a startled scream escapes me, and when I whirl around to see who it is, my knees give out.

It's Dad. And he's pointing a gun at me.

CHAPTER 4

I have so many questions, but my brain won't form words.

Dad is here, and he's going to kill me. I'm certain of that.

"Lissy, be quiet," he urges, pressing a finger to his lips. The other hand holds tightly onto the gun, and I stare down its barrel. I've never seen a gun in my life, much less had one pointed at me. By my own father.

My breath comes in short bursts. I don't know what to do.

Where is Mom? Why isn't she home yet?

"Don't be scared, honey," he says softly. That's when I notice Harper next to him, pale as a ghost, her whole body trembling. "Show me where Levi is, and then come with me."

Oh my God, Levi. Fire burns within my chest. "Please don't hurt us," I squeak.

Dad's face actually falls, like I've wounded him with my words. "I'm not going to hurt any of you. Please, just let me see Levi. I'll explain. And give me your phones."

Fuck. Harper and I share a terrified glance, and I know we're thinking the same thing as we hesitantly place our phones in his outstretched palm: there's no amount of explaining he can do to justify *this*. This can't be real.

Dad leads us through the living room toward the stairs, and the vaulted ceilings above my head spin as white-hot panic takes over me. Would Dad actually shoot us? Maybe he's just trying to scare us into giving him what he wants, but what *does* he want? I don't want to find the answer the hard way, so I obediently climb the stairs until I'm at Levi's closed door, the cold metal of the gun pressed against my spine. I give a light knock. "Levi, open the door please."

"Is it safe?" Levi says from the other side, and Dad's features deflate, like he might cry.

"Yes," I lie.

The door creaks open, and when Levi emerges, his face lights up at the sight of Dad. It's been months since any of us have seen him; maybe three? Four? "Daddy!" he cries as he opens his arms wide, oblivious to the gun.

A hint of a smile crosses Dad's face. He slings an arm around Levi's shoulder. "Hey, buddy. Your sisters and I are about to go somewhere special. You're coming with us."

"Where are we going?"

"It's a surprise."

Reality hits me like a cold, hard slap. Dad is about to kidnap us. Oh my God, he's going to kidnap us. He's going to take us to some super-secret location and kill us to get back at Mom for making that video about him. Where the fuck is she, and why isn't she here to stop this?

I guess we'll have to save ourselves. I wrack my brain for ways I can stall him, but I come up with nothing.

"Can I bring Snuggles?" Levi gestures to his favourite teddy bear; the filthy, tattered one that should've been thrown out years ago.

"Go ahead, but make it quick. We need to get going."

Levi scoops the bear up in his arms, and that's when his gaze falls on the gun. At first, he freezes, like he doesn't understand what he's seeing, but then he screams as loud as his lungs will allow him, and the sound somehow brings me relief. We don't have neighbours, but a part of me hopes someone walking by might hear and call the police.

It's a stretch, I know. But a girl can hope.

He tries to run back into the room, but Dad grabs him by the arm and forces him backward. "Stop screaming," he demands. "You're coming with me. And if any of you scream again, there will be consequences."

Levi whimpers, and his face twists. Harper and I nod in unison. What those consequences are, I have no idea, but I'm not ready to find out.

We walk single file down the spiral staircase and back through the living room toward the front door. I take one last look around, at our backpacks lying in a heap by the door, at the episode of SpongeBob SquarePants playing on the flatscreen TV, and wonder if we'll ever see this house again. If we'll ever have another family movie night in this living room. If I'll ever finish reading the book I've left on my bedside table. If I'll ever get back in the driver's seat of my Civic Mom bought me two months ago. My lungs seize at the thought. I used to think I wanted to leave this place to get away from the vlog, but not like this.

I'd rather bow down to every one of Mom's demands for the vlog than be threatened by my father.

A wave of heat washes over me as we step outside into the hot, early-summer air. Dad's black BMW is parked along the curb out front. "The doors are unlocked," he tells us. "Get in the back."

As we crawl in, I wonder if I'm being weak by not fighting back. I should be braver than this. The characters in my books never let a gun scare them, especially when they have younger siblings to protect. Dammit, why can't I be like those badass female characters? The only thing I can manage to do as Dad climbs in is blurt, "Where are we going?"

Dad guns it down our street; a driving style I've never seen from him. "I can't tell you yet, Lissy. You'll see when we get there."

"Can you at least tell me how far away we're going?"

"No."

His response makes my blood boil, and I stare out the window while Harper and Levi sniffle next to me. Hopefully I'll see Mom's car. Sawyer is a pretty small town; with any luck, someone will recognize Dad's car and wonder what he's doing here, maybe even call Mom to gossip about it. It might be the only time gossip could ever be beneficial in my life.

"Daddy, I wanna go home," Levi whines. There's snot dribbling from his nose, and some of it lands on Snuggles.

"I know, buddy." Dad turns left at the stoplight, and just like that, we're speeding down the highway and leaving Sawyer. Nothing but trees surround us now. "But I'm bringing you to your new home, and I think you'll like it a lot better. There's even *lots* of Legos in the basement just for you."

Dad definitely isn't bringing us to his own house; that would be too obvious. The thought sends a whole new wave of fear through me; what if the police never find us? What if we'll never be able to escape? I want to throw up.

"I just don't understand why you're doing this," I say. I steal another glance out the window; are we driving too fast for me to jump out and go get help? "You're kidnapping us."

Harper wails at the word *kidnap*. "We're gonna die!"

"I needed to get you away from that toxic environment," Dad says after a beat. "This is for your own safety. I know you guys don't want to leave, but someday you'll look back to this moment and thank me. I promise."

Thank him? What the fuck?

The car suddenly feels too small. The walls are closing in on me. The seatbelt is too tight across my chest. I need to get out. Now.

I'm reaching for the seatbelt when Dad's voice filters in through the noise in my head. "Lissy, what are you doing?"

"Let me out!" The ferocity of my voice startles me. "Pull over right now and let me out."

A sigh. "I'm not—"

"LET ME OUT!"

"No!"

"You're kidnapping us!"

"Daddy, I'm scared," Levi whimpers.

"I'm keeping you safe!" Dad roars. "Your mother is putting you in danger with that vlog. She doesn't care about any of you, and she should never have gotten full custody. The courts are fucking stupid. But don't worry, you'll never have to see her again."

"She's going to find us." My voice drips with venom. I try to tell myself this is what being brave looks like. "When she sees that we're gone, she'll do everything she can to get us back."

His gaze meets mine in the rearview mirror, and his eyes flash with anger. "She's a narcissist. I'm sure you three being gone will get her *tons* of views. Consider this the last favour I'll ever do for her."

Frustrated tears well in my eyes. Dad's crazy; Mom is not that heartless. When she sees that we're gone and checks the doorbell camera…God, it's going to destroy her. Everything she said about Dad in her last video comes rushing back, and I choke back a sob. He really is a monster. But he's right about one thing; Mom *will* get tons of views on the next video she makes. And she won't be making it with the intent to cash in on us being missing; she'll use it to get as many people as possible to help find us.

How long that will take, I have no idea. I'll find us a way out in the meantime. But I'm going to put all my trust into Mom and our viewers to get us home as quickly as possible.

CHAPTER 5

The moment Dad steers the BMW down the winding dirt road, I know exactly where we're going.

It's been years since any of us have been out here; Levi is too young to remember, since he was just a baby. But I see the flash of recognition in Harper's eyes as well, and she bursts into tears for the fifth time in the three hours we've been in the car. She knows, too, just how far in the middle of nowhere we are.

We're going to the cottage.

When we were little, Mom and Dad bought a small cottage on the water and would take us camping there a few times a year. Some of my earliest memories take place at this cottage; I remember spending hours playing in the water with Harper, teaching her how to swim, jumping off the dock, doing underwater handstands, playing badminton in the grass. There were two other cottages on either side of us, and we'd play with the kids who stayed there all day long. Keely, Summer, Brayden, and Jack…I wonder if they still come out here sometimes, if their parents still own these cottages. Maybe they'd recognize that we're in trouble.

But Mom and Dad sold this cottage the year after Levi was born. How did Dad get it back? And wouldn't Mom remember this place and tell the police to check here?

For the first time in the three-hour drive, a hint of a smile crosses my face. It might be a bit of a long shot, but if Mom pushes aside the fact that they sold the cottage, maybe she'll send the police out to come get us and we'll be home by tomorrow. Dad will end up in jail for being too dumb to come up with a better kidnapping plot.

The car kicks up clouds of dust as we drive up the bumpy road, and the occasional rock pelts the windshield. Harper reaches for my hand, and I squeeze it tight, reassuring her that I'll keep her safe. Aside from her crying, we're all silent for the rest of the drive.

There's a sharp bend in the road, and Dad steers the car left. The cottage is right after this corner. My heart pounds in my throat as we get closer, and I spot the roof through a small clearing in the trees. There's a Corolla in the driveway. I freeze; Dad isn't working alone. Who else is here? A new girlfriend? A coworker?

Dad doesn't slow down, and he sails right by the cottage and its neighbours.

Ice washes over my body. We're clearly not going to the cottage, but if I ask Dad any more questions, his temper will come out in full force. I only have my imagination to rely on now.

The road winds the further we travel, and dozens of stunning cottages line the right side of the street. The rain has stopped, but the clouds are dark, ominous, threatening a storm. I rest my head against the window and watch the trees roll by as we drive. I imagine that we're embarking on a quiet summer vacation with Dad, taking a break from the cameras, spending some quality time together without monetizing it. It temporarily helps me forget the unknown that awaits us when this car finally stops.

Soon we're pulling into the driveway of a different cottage. It's much smaller than our old one, with stained white siding and two tiny windows facing the driveway. There's a wooden sign by the green door with "The Bucknells" carved into it. "Well, we made it," Dad says as he throws the car in park. "This is home for the next little while."

I stare at the sign. "This isn't your cottage. Who are the Bucknells?"

"My coworker owns it," Dad says, beaming. "Come on, let's go check it out."

Harper and Levi hesitantly unbuckle their seatbelts, but I stay put. "Does he know we're staying here?"

"No. He barely uses it, so he lets some of the guys at work have copies of the keys so they can come whenever they want."

This knowledge soothes my nerves a little. If someone else owns it and other people have keys, that means we can't stay here forever. Summer break is just about to start; someone surely will want to take their kids here at some point. Maybe this won't be so bad, after all.

"Come on, guys. Get inside."

We slide out of the car and follow Dad inside. He's still holding the gun, but doesn't point it at us, just lets it hang at his side. He doesn't need to use it; where will we run to? The nearest neighbour is at least an hour-long walk from here

The cottage smells musty, and the hardwood floors creak as we step in the door. Dad deposits the keys on a shelf along the kitchen wall and leads us to a white door with mold stains by the hinges. I fight off the urge to gag. "I'm sorry, guys," he says as he opens it, "but you're going to be staying down here, in the basement. For your own safety."

My skin prickles. "You can't lock us in a basement."

"I can. Now go."

"No, I don't want to," says Levi, clutching his teddy bear tighter. "It's dark."

Dad places a hand on Levi's back and shoves him forward with more force than necessary. "I don't care if you don't want to. You're safe. That's all that matters." He flips the light switch on, bathing the room in a yellow glow. "Get moving."

We descend into the basement, Dad following. The steps groan beneath our feet, protesting our arrival, and Dad shuts the basement door behind him. Chills dance across my arms; it's freezing down here. I suddenly wish I'd opted to wear a hoodie today instead of this thin t-shirt, but then again, how was I supposed to know I'd be locked in a cold basement in the middle of a heatwave?

I glance around the basement, my new home for who knows how long. Three air mattresses, arranged neatly with blankets and pillows, line the wall straight ahead. An open door to the left reveals a tiny bathroom with a glass shower that I'm not even sure I'd fit in. The Legos Dad promised lay scattered across the floor to the right, as if the box had been spilled. There is one small window, and the sight sends a thrill through me; we might be able to escape through that window.

Dad orders us to sit on the mattresses, and as I lower myself down, Harper lets out another scream that makes me jump. She bolts back up the steps before Dad can stop her and frantically tries the doorknob, but it's locked. "Help!" She pounds on the door with both fists, the sound booming through the small space. "Please help! Someone!"

"Harper, enough!" Dad storms up the steps, and my breath hitches in my throat. He picks her up around her middle, and she flails in his arms, kicking and punching at dead air. "No one can hear you."

"Let me out!" she wails. "Please. I want to go home! I want Mom!"

"Just let me explain!"

He drops down into a nearby chair and holds her tightly in his lap. She's panting hard, and her dark hair sticks to her face, but she doesn't brush it away. "I brought you here because your safety is the last thing on your mother's mind," Dad starts. "She doesn't—"

I scoff. "You keep saying that word. 'Safety.' How exactly are we safe here? You kidnapped us at gunpoint."

I almost miss it, but Dad flinches a little. I've struck a bit of a nerve, I guess. "I brought it in case your mother was home. She'd never have let me take you. And I know it scared you, but how else was I supposed to get you to come with me?"

"That doesn't really explain anything."

He wrings his hands together. "Her video sparked a lot of outrage online. And I'd be deserving of it, if the things she said were true. But they weren't. I've been getting nonstop death threats since, and I know for sure that there are people after me. I basically have to go into hiding. That, and your mom has been exploiting you three for money since you were born, and that kind of environment is not good for you."

Mom definitely wasn't lying about some of the things she mentioned in the video; as long as I can remember, Dad would call us names when he was upset, and he'd make fun of Mom as soon as her hands reached for the vlog camera. *Time to tell the internet I'm taking a dump!* he'd say mockingly. I'd be lying if I didn't secretly say the same thing under my breath every time that damn lens pointed in my direction. But what about all the other points she made in her video?

"You didn't drain the money out of Mom's account?" Harper asks, beating me to the question.

He shakes his head and squeezes Harper a little tighter. "No. I would never do that. At the end of the day, she was using that money to provide for you, and I'd never take something like that away from her."

"Well, she didn't lie about you calling us names." My voice is barely above a whisper, but he still hears me.

He visibly sags at my words. "I know, and I'm sorry. I have no excuses for that. But you're better off staying here with me."

"So, because you need to go into hiding, we need to go into hiding too? What kind of life is that for us?"

He sighs, clearly frustrated. "We're not staying here forever. You won't be in *hiding* for very long."

"How are we gonna go to school?" says Levi.

"We'll figure it out."

"You've been wanting me to go to a good college since birth," I argue. "I can't go to college trapped out here."

"There are virtual options."

"What if I wanted to be a doctor? Or a mechanic? I can't learn all of that remotely. That's impossible."

He rises to his feet and places Harper back on the floor. "I'm going upstairs to make dinner. We'll talk more about this later." He angles his body towards the stairs and starts his way back up. "But I'm making it clear right now; I'm not bringing you back to that house. Ever again."

He slams the door behind him, and the walls rattle. The lock clicks in place. We're alone now.

"Alyssa?" Levi grabs my arm. "I'm scared."

"What are we gonna do?" says Harper.

"I don't know." I stand a little straighter. "But one thing's for sure; we're going to get out of here. Help me come up with a plan."

NEW VIDEO FROM THEBENNETTFAM
PLEASE HELP

Hey everyone, it's Melissa. Sorry if I sound out of breath, but I need your help, desperately. And no, this video is not clickbait, nor is it a prank. In fact, I've demonetized this video. I'll just cut right to the chase; my kids are missing.

They've been kidnapped by Dan.

This is every mother's worst nightmare. Oh God.

Just a few hours ago, I came home from the store, and the kids were gone. At first, I thought Alyssa was just late coming home, but after half an hour of no one answering my calls, I decided to check our doorbell cam. And that's when I saw Dan approach our front door with a gun in his hand. He pointed it right at Harper when she answered the door and...oh my God, this is so hard to talk about.

He took all the kids out of the house at gunpoint and loaded them into his car and just...left with them. So I'm going to show you the doorbell cam footage in the hopes that one of you guys, even though it's a bit of a longshot, might see this man or this car and call the police right away.

CLIP PLAYS

In case you can't see it clearly enough, the car is a black 2021 BMW X6 with license plate DB1019. It's an Ontario license plate. Dan is wearing a black hoodie that looks like it has the Carhartt logo on one sleeve, and blue jeans. Alyssa is wearing a white v-neck t-shirt with light blue cutoff denim shorts. Harper is wearing a dark blue jumpsuit with white flowers. Levi is wearing a plain black t-shirt and khaki shorts.

If ANYONE sees them, please call 911 immediately. The police are already doing everything they can, and an Amber Alert has been sent *out, but I'll take all the help I can get. There are 4.3 million of you. I'm really hoping at least one of you might know something. Maybe you have an idea where he's taken them. If you do, please drop a comment. I'm going to be reading them all, and at the same time, I'm going to be out everywhere looking for my babies. I just...I don't know what I'll ever do without them. It's only been a couple hours, and I'm so sick to my stomach.*

Someone has to know something. Please help me.

CHAPTER 6
LAST YEAR

In an alternate universe, I'd be flattered that the popular girls stopped at my table during lunch to talk to me. My heart would be beating out of my chest as I nodded along to their words, secretly begging them to like me, to let me hang out with them, to think I'm cool. I'd do *anything* to get their validation for five minutes. Pathetic, right?

In this universe, I'm fucking terrified of them. Because if they're willingly talking to me, that means there's something wrong.

Cara and I are at our usual spot in the cafeteria, in the back right corner, comparing the number of books we've read this week, when I see them eyeing me from afar. Laurel Sanders, the group's leader, is whispering something in Jessica Yaworski's ear, and Jessica keeps her gaze trained on me, snickering. My stomach burns. I try to turn back to my conversation with Cara, but then the girls are making a beeline straight to our table, and the air rushes right out of my lungs.

Cara doesn't notice. She's clutching a copy of the newest addition to her Colleen Hoover collection—Layla—and talking animatedly about its contents. "Could you imagine getting to talk to a ghost! Like, imagine I died, and I used Laurel's body to talk to you. Would you tolerate her a little better after that?"

"Cara."

She ignores me. "You can borrow this after I'm done with it. You *have* to read it. I promise you'll love it."

She already knows Mom won't let me read Colleen Hoover's books because there are sex scenes in them. And right now, I don't give a shit about Colleen Hoover's books. I give a shit about the fact that Laurel and Jessica are on their way to humiliate me once again, and their reason for it this time remains unknown.

"Hey, girly." Laurel deposits her hand on my shoulder, and I bristle. "How's it going?"

Cara drops her book on the table. "Leave her alone," she snarls. "She doesn't want to talk to you."

"Then she can use her words and tell me to go away." Laurel leans closer and directs her attention back to me. "But I just thought I'd let you know that you're not very good at keeping things secret. I saw your mom's last video. Everyone knows you have a massive crush on Blake."

If I were standing, my knees would've buckled, and I'd have collapsed to the floor. My mouth turns sour. White hot panic grips me. I've never admitted to having a crush on Blake out loud before, not even to Cara. How did they find out? Is it really that obvious?

I want to disappear.

"Don't even try to deny it," says Jessica. "You don't need to embarrass yourself any more than you already have."

"And Blake is definitely not your type," Laurel adds.

"No one asked for your opinion." Cara stands. "We're leaving, Alyssa."

"No." My own voice surprises me. They don't get to win this time; I'm not going to run out of the cafeteria like a coward. "Watching a ten-minute video doesn't mean you know me."

"Oh yeah?" Laurel challenges. "So if I call Blake over right now, that won't bother you?"

Fuck.

My stomach clenches. *I can't do this I can't do this I can't do this.*
I could kill Mom right now.

The video in question: in honour of Valentine's Day, Mom made a video recounting the story of how she and Dad first met in high school. They'd gone to the Spring Fling dance with their friends, and Dad accidentally spilled his Root Beer on Mom's white dress. And the rest is history. It's a cute story, but once Mom got to the end, she decided to tell our viewers that there's a boy I'm eyeing at school, and maybe I should ask him out one day. She didn't mention a name. But apparently Laurel and Jessica figured out who it is.

I make a mental note to never tell Mom anything ever again.

"You don't need to do that," I squeak. "Really. It was just a stupid video and she never said—"

"Blake!" Laurel hollers, whirling to face him. The cafeteria falls silent.

He looks up at the sound of his name, and *ugh*, he's beautiful. Those high cheekbones, chocolate brown eyes, blindingly white teeth...something about his presence just demands to be noticed at all times, as if a spotlight is permanently gleaming over him. He's so perfect it hurts. I don't know how he doesn't have a girlfriend yet, considering it's been three whole months since Melodie Templeton dumped him. My heart tugs; I want *so* badly for him to be mine. He just has to notice me first.

Ideally, not this way.

Laurel waves him over to our table. "Come here. I need to ask you something."

"Please," I beg. I hate that I'm begging. "I promise it's not him. Why do you care so much? It's not him, Laurel. Please."

Too late; Blake is already striding across the cafeteria toward us, an amused smile crossing his lips. I try not to stare at the muscles poking through his plain white t-shirt as he walks. Instead, I focus on the bone-deep existential dread that weighs heavy as a rock in the centre of my stomach.

But maybe something good will come out of this. Maybe he'll stare lovingly into my blue eyes and admit that he's had a crush on me this whole time, that he thinks I'm the most beautiful girl on the planet, that we should catch dinner and a movie later this week. He'll tell Laurel and Jessica to get lost, and their shocked expressions will make my day, maybe even my whole year.

Reality hits me like a freight train as Blake himself arrives at my table. And then what would happen? We'd ride off together into the sunset like two star-crossed lovers? What the fuck is wrong with me? Am I really that delusional?

Blake stares expectantly at Laurel. "You wanted to ask me something?"

"No, she didn't," says Cara. "She just wants to be a bitch. You can leave."

"Shut up." Laurel barks out a laugh. "I just wanted to know if you were aware that Alyssa has a massive crush on you?"

Heat rises to my cheeks, and I shrink in my seat. I find a smudge of ketchup on the table and stare at it. Maybe if I stare long enough, all sound around me will disappear, and I won't hear what they're saying. I can't look at any of them.

Unsurprisingly, that doesn't work. Blake's cheeks turn pink. "Um."

"Yeah." Jessica sneers. "She tells her mom all about you. She even made a Valentine's Day video talking about how obsessed she is with you and how badly she wants to have sex with you. And—"

"Stop!" I protest. "That's not true!"

"—she wants you to ask her out. But it has to be an expensive candlelight dinner, and she needs to vlog the whole thing so she can brag to all her fans that she has a boyfriend."

"No, I—"

"The video already has a million views. So now a million people know that she's in love with you. Do you love her back?"

God, this is so awkward. The corner of his lip curls ever so slightly in a look of…disgust? It's so subtle I almost miss it. I brace myself for his answer, knowing exactly what's to come.

"It's okay, you can say it," Laurel says to him. "You don't owe her anything. So, do you like her or not?"

His eyes soften as he finally acknowledges my existence. "I'm sorry, Alyssa," he says quietly. "I just…don't feel the same. I don't really know you that well. And, to be honest, it kind of makes me a little uncomfortable that you put my name out there for the whole internet to talk about."

Just like that, the ground rips out from beneath my feet. He didn't even try to ask whether or not it was true. He doesn't want to hear my side of the story. People are staring now, and the laughter that follows is a tidal wave washing over my head, forcing me beneath the surface. I can't breathe. I have to get out of here before I drown.

I abruptly stand and bolt toward the bathroom doors, choking on air. I promised myself I wouldn't let them win, but what else was I supposed to do? I might have online popularity, but here in these hallways, I'm no one. I close myself into a stall and with shaking hands, I dial Dad's number. He'll know what to do.

"Hey Lissy," he says on the second ring. "What's up?"

Before I can get any words out, I'm sobbing. This is so unfair. Everyone hates me, and I can't even begin to understand why. "I want to come home," I blubber. "Can you come pick me up?"

"What's going on?" His tone softens.

The bathroom door bangs open, and then Cara is calling my name. She'll have to wait. "Everyone's making fun of me," I whimper. "I can't be here anymore."

"Making fun of you?"

"Yeah." I sniffle. "The whole cafeteria just started laughing at me and—"

"I'm on my way, sweetheart. It's okay. We'll talk about it when I get there."

He hangs up then. As I wait for Dad to come to the rescue, I decide it's only fair to let Cara in, considering she's making a scene. When she sees my face, she winces. "Alyssa. You're seriously going home?"

"Now's not the time for a lecture." I catch a glimpse of myself in the mirror behind her and get a jump scare; mascara runs down my red, blotchy face, and my eyes are swollen. I look like I've just stepped out of a serious boxing match.

"They're assholes." Cara kicks the stall door, and the bang erupts through the small space. "You know why they treat you like this? It's because they want to *be* you. They want what you have."

I snort. "They want to be a loser?"

"No. You know what I mean. They want to be internet famous. Rich."

"Well, they can have it. Because I'm tired of it."

My phone chimes; Dad's here. That was quick. "Gotta go." I show her the text. "My dad's waiting for me. I'll see you tomorrow."

"Okay. Feel better, I guess."

I drag my feet as I walk away. Cara is annoyed, I can tell, and I can't stand to have any more people judging my every move. I choke on a sob. She'll never understand what this feels like.

Dad is standing in the main office when I get there, and we don't say a word to each other until we get to the car. "So, what happened?" he asks as he backs out of the parking spot, his hand resting on the back of my seat.

I swallow. "In Mom's Valentine's Day video, she talked about this guy I like, and everyone at school figured out who it was. So they told him."

Dad shakes his head slowly and lets out a sigh. "I'm sorry, Lissy."

"It's not your—"

"I know. But I'm going to have a talk with your mother when we get home. Some things need to be private. She doesn't always see that."

"I just hate how every aspect of my life is being used for *content*." I throw my head back against the headrest. "It's not fun anymore. No one cares what I ate for breakfast this morning. No one cares that I stubbed my toe and now I have a bruise. *No one cares* that I have a crush on some guy that doesn't like me back. No one cares except random eight-year-olds who will never meet me watching our videos on their iPads."

I'm crying again, but shit, my chest feels so much lighter now that I've spoken those words aloud. It's not exactly a secret that I hate our channel, but the naïve part of my brain hopes that Dad can use this knowledge to convince Mom to stop. They argue about the channel all the time. Maybe this will be the final straw.

"I know." Dad says it so quietly, I almost don't hear him. "It's not fair to you, or to Harper and Levi. If you don't want to do this, that decision should be respected, not challenged. Let me talk to her. Because it pains me to watch you three go through this, and I don't know how much longer I can stand it."

I hug my knees to my chest and choke out a weak "Thank you." The relief—although temporary—is overwhelming.

CHAPTER 7
NOW

In books, they make coming up with escape plans sound easy. But the more I stare at these four barren walls, the more I'm starting to doubt our options.

We don't really *have* options. But Harper and Levi aren't allowed to know that.

"Is Daddy coming back?" Levi whispers from the corner. He's sitting cross-legged on one of the mattresses, a plaid blanket draped over his head. He wraps it around his body as if he's shielding himself from this day.

"Soon, but I don't know when." I take another glance around the room. "While he's gone, we need to start planning how the heck we're going to get out of here."

I glance outside. It's still gloomy, and droplets of leftover rain stick to the glass. Harper follows my gaze. "Can we fit through that window?"

I get up and move closer to it. It's too high up—we'd need to find something to stand on to get up there—but it doesn't look large enough to fit a human body through. It's narrow and rectangular. Fortunately, it doesn't have bars on it like I've seen in some movies. "I don't know if we'll fit," I say honestly, folding my arms across my chest. "And even if we could, how do we break it without Dad hearing?"

She harrumphs. "We don't. Maybe we'll just have to break it during the day, crawl through it as fast as we can, and run. We're probably faster than him."

"That's not very realistic, Harper. He has a gun *and* a car, two things we don't have."

"Well, what do you want me to say? Do you have any bright ideas, then, SmartyPants?"

My body prickles with irritation. "Look, we don't have time to argue. We need to do something, or else we'll be down here forever. He clearly has no intentions of letting us go."

"I don't wanna be trapped down here forever," says Levi.

"Exactly. So we need to act fast."

Harper bounces nervously on her mattress and fidgets with the hair elastic around her wrist. She's getting just as antsy as I am. "What if, when Dad comes down next, we run past him? Or we distract him somehow? He might leave it unlocked when he comes down here."

I shake my head. "I don't think we can count on that either. We could try, but at this point, the window might be our best option."

"But you said we can't fit through it."

"We won't know until we try."

A lightbulb goes off in my head, blinding me with relief. We could make him leave the cottage while we work on breaking the window so he doesn't hear us. I'll just say I need something, like tampons. "I think I've figured it out," I say.

I dash to the bathroom, my lungs squeezing. I rip open the cabinet doors, and to my horror, there's already a box of tampons sitting there. I don't know whether to be impressed that he's so prepared for us or devastated. My heart sinks. But wait; I could ask for pads. Harper doesn't use tampons.

"What are you doing in there?" Harper demands.

"We can ask him to leave," I tell her proudly. "We'll tell him we need something, and he'll go get it for us. Then we can break the window without him hearing us."

She scoffs. "But the police probably know he's the one who took us. He'll get arrested the second he's seen in public."

Fuck, she's right. "But he's eventually going to need to go to the store for something, like groceries. Unless he has someone else doing that for him. Ugh, the more we talk about this, the more hopeless it feels."

"We could pretend to be hurt." Harper holds her foot and pretends to wince in pain. "'*Dad, I tripped and I think I broke my ankle. Take me to the hospital.*' You know how good I am at crying on cue."

I leave the bathroom and collapse onto the mattress next to Levi, heaving a sigh. Levi sighs, too. "Even if we're hurt, whether real or fake, Dad will do everything in his power to avoid a hospital," I say to the ceiling. "Unless we're at a risk of dying—like a stroke or heart attack—he's going to try and treat it himself here. The whole country will be looking for us, so it'd be game over for him to take us anywhere."

"Shit."

"Don't swear, Harper. You're eleven."

"And? What are you gonna do about it?"

I shake my head. "Forget it. Let's just try to break the window."

The sight of a window in this prison-like basement is both beautiful and intimidating. It might be the only way out. The longer I stare at it, the more I realize that Levi is the only one who has a chance of fitting through it. There aren't neighbours for miles, and that's too far for a seven-year-old to walk by himself. The deep dark of the woods bordering the murky water of the lake would swallow him whole. It's also the home of bears, coyotes, wolves, moose…the thought of sending my little brother out there alone sends a shudder through me. I couldn't live with myself if something happened to him out there.

If—when—we leave, we go together. It would be almost just as dangerous to leave someone behind. If Dad came downstairs and didn't see all of us, I don't want to imagine what he'd do.

I can't say he won't hurt us. I would've thought otherwise if he hadn't come through our front door aiming a gun at his own children. It feels as though I don't know this man anymore, what he's capable of. He admitted he never intends to shoot us, but how do I know he didn't say that to calm us down?

Anger climbs through my veins, slowly at first, then it floods to the surface like water crashing through a dam. I don't care if I won't fit through the window; I need to make it work. Dad doesn't deserve to keep us for a second longer. I'm going to get us home, and after we get there, I never want to see his pathetic face again. Consider him dead to me.

I slam my hands against the mattress and bolt to my feet. Thunder rumbles outside, distant at first, then it grows to a bass-like roar. There's a faded blue tote box tucked near the furnace, and I storm over to it, ripping off the lid. With any luck, there will be something sharp enough to break the glass. Tools, if the universe was really on my side. But as I sift through the box's contents, I mostly find camping supplies: kindling wood, skewers, paper plates, tongs…useless stuff. Shouldn't there be an axe somewhere?

I laugh to myself. Of course, Dad would've taken the axe away if there had been one down here. That would've been too easy.

"What are you doing?" Harper kneels next to me, peering into the box.

"Help me find something to break the window."

She furrows her brow. "I thought you said—"

"Are you going to help me or not?"

She reaches a hand inside. "Fine. But it doesn't look like there's anything in here."

"Keep looking."

We tear apart the inside of the box, yanking every object out so we don't miss anything. Before long, the floor is a mess. Another loud clap of thunder booms overhead, and the lights flicker. "Alyssa, I'm scared," Levi calls out.

I don't have time for this right now. "Tuck yourself under the blanket until it's over," I say. "We're safe. The basement is the safest place you can be in a storm."

It seems to work, because he's quiet after that. When the box is nearly empty, I pace the furnace room, searching for anything else that may be hiding somewhere; another tote box, maybe. But then I see it, and an idea takes shape in my head.

A stainless steel lunch box, perched on the middle shelf. It might not be perfect, but it'll be heavy enough to break the glass.

I rush over to it and cradle it in my trembling hands, the cold seeping through my fingers. I'll swing this thing as hard as I can at that glass, and it'll explode. Tears spring to my eyes. "I found what we need," I tell Harper. "Now we just need to reach the window. Grab that Lego box and put it underneath. I'm going to stand on it."

She follows me out of the furnace room and scoots the Lego box under the window. It wobbles beneath my feet at first, and I steady myself against the concrete wall. "Wait, what's the plan for after we break it?" Harper asks. "We can't just break it without a plan."

A flash of lightning blinds me, and the orange glow sticks to the corners of my vision. "We go out youngest to oldest. Line up behind me. Once it's open, I'll lift Levi through, then you, then I'll go out last."

"In this storm? Is that even safe?"

"I don't care." And it's true; any fear I may have ever had over thunderstorms vanishes. "Maybe there's a shed nearby we can hide in until it blows over. But we have to start running. Stay hidden in the trees and, I can't stress this enough, *do not* go near the road. That'll be the first place Dad goes once he realizes we're gone. We'll have to stick close enough to the road that we can follow it, but far enough away that no one will see us. Got it?"

"Should we check if Dad left any extra clothes for us down here?" Harper pretends to shiver. "We're going to be so cold and wet. I want a sweater."

"Go look, then," I snap. We don't really have time to look for extra clothes, but whatever. "And hurry."

She disappears into the furnace room and emerges a minute later with three hoodies in her arms. "Bingo. Put these on."

She hands one to each of us; they're matching royal blue hoodies with "Lake Erie" printed in bold letters across the front. I shrug mine on, and gradually the goosebumps on my arms disappear. It's a smart choice, one I should give Harper credit for. We don't know how long we'll be out there, and we certainly don't want hypothermia to kick in.

I steal a glance over my shoulder at my siblings. "Ready?"

They both nod, and I suck in a large breath; I can't mess this up. Dad may not hear the glass shattering over the storm, so I have to do this now. I grit my teeth and hold the lunch box over my shoulder, ready for action. *Three, two...*

Another bolt of lightning. The lights go out, and the room plunges into darkness.

I swing anyway.

For a moment, the room is eerily silent, but when the lunch box connects with the glass, the sound of the crack is almost deafening. It doesn't explode like I imagined, but a spiderweb of cracks dances across the surface, and a small hole forms in the middle. A cool breeze trickles through it. I just have to keep swinging and—

The basement door opens.

CHAPTER 8

"I really didn't want to do this," says Dad as he secures the rope around my wrists, pulling it tight until it squeezes against my bones. "Please believe me."

I grit my teeth against the pain. "Fuck you."

Before today, I wouldn't dare dream of swearing at my father, but I think I've earned it. He's tied each of us to a basement beam, and we writhe on the cold floor, darkness surrounding us. Levi sobs in the corner, complaining that the rope is hurting him, that it's digging into his skin, but Dad says nothing for a long time. I see his silhouette pacing in front of us.

"I don't want you to be scared of me," he finally says, addressing us all. He wipes his palms on his jeans. "But you need to be punished for what you did. This isn't my cottage; it's Pete's. You broke *his* window, and now I have to pay to fix it. Until I can get it fixed, it's going to be awfully cold down here with that hole in the glass. You have yourselves to blame for that."

Pete. The name sounds familiar. I push the thought aside for now. "You don't want us to be scared of you. But you tied up your own children."

"You left me no other choice!" he roars. "And you know what? Your mom has conditioned you all to hate me, to fear me. That ends now. I'm so *goddamn* tired of being villainized when all I've ever done is love you guys."

"So it's Mom's fault you tied us up?" I thrash against the rope, seeing red. I was so close to getting us out of here. But I was too impulsive, and now the plan is ruined. How are we ever going to escape?

"I'm not saying it's her fault I tied you up. But it's her fault for endangering you. If I didn't take you, some crazy stalker eventually would have."

"If you let us go, we'll make Mom quit," Harper begs. "*Please.* She'll do whatever you want, trust me. Just let us go, and I'll never let her film us ever again if she tries."

"Harper, sweetie, you know she won't do that." Dad's voice softens.

"Yes she will! You're scaring her enough right now. She'll do anything."

"She lied about me for internet views. Now let's say, in theory, I bring you back right now. What makes you think she won't make ten more videos talking about everything that's unfolded today, exploiting your story for money?"

He has a point, but Harper is more than likely right. My insides crumble, and I squeeze my eyes shut. I still can't believe this is really happening, that this isn't some wild dream I'll wake up from and tell everyone about. The failed chemistry exam pales in comparison to what's happened today. It almost feels silly that I worried about a piece of paper in the first place, that I wasted space in my brain stressing over something that doesn't matter in the long run. I even had the audacity to take everything I had for granted; a beautiful house. Money. Fans. Multiple vacations a year. My own car. Books. An excellent education. A supportive best friend. A Mom who loved me.

We might not leave this basement for a long time, so we'll have to learn to live without those things. A tear trickles down my cheek. I hope Mom knows how much I love her, despite how I've treated her recently. I've been nothing but a spoiled brat.

At the start of the afternoon, there was comfort in the fact that Dad seemed to be flying by the seat of his pants, making things up as he went along, but I'm starting to think this took months of planning. Maybe a year. Mom's video must have tipped him over the edge and made him kick the plan into action sooner than he'd intended.

"What about your job?" I ask him. "Aren't they going to wonder where you are?"

The lights flicker back on, and the room is bathed in a yellow glow. "I quit my job last night," he says. "I've got plenty saved to last us for a few months, but I'm going to find another job working from home under a new identity."

I shiver; he *really* did his homework. "And food? How are you getting that?"

"Pete."

"But you said Pete didn't know we were here." My heart drops into my stomach. This probably means Pete doesn't give copies of the keys to other coworkers like Dad said, so no other families will be coming here to save us. How could someone want to help Dad pull this off?

Dad sighs. "He does. I panicked a bit when you first asked me. There was no way I could do this alone."

He bends down and snakes his arm around my shoulders. My body stiffens. "All three of you need to know how sorry I am. It will get better, I promise. Once the news dies down a bit, we'll have a little more freedom and might even get to go on a trip. I know being locked down here won't feel like much of a life to you. But it won't be forever."

He may believe that now, but there are 4.3 million people around the world who will recognize us in a heartbeat, no matter how long we've been missing. Not to mention the thousands of people who've never heard of us that will be watching the news. I force air into my lungs as he holds me, plants a kiss on my cheek, then does the same for Harper and Levi. Harper visibly recoils.

"I'm going to go upstairs now," he says carefully. "I need you three to think for a while about what you did. I'll be back with dinner."

Then he leaves us. The stairs creak beneath his feet as he walks away, the sound grating my ears. Then the door closes behind him. The click of the lock reminds me of my failure.

"What are we gonna do now?" Harper whispers.

I can't even look at her. "I wish I knew."

***

Three hours later, the basement door swings open, and the smell of barbeque fills the room. Normally we'd have eaten hours ago—it's probably close to ten o'clock at night now—but despite that, I'm not hungry. Nausea swirls in the pit of my stomach instead. I'll admit, the food smells lovely, but what if he's drugged it?

Dad sets a burger down in front of me; only ketchup, just the way I like it. He reaches for my wrist and cuts the rope free, and I breathe a sigh of relief at the release. Dad winces at the deep red marks left on my skin. "Does that hurt, Lissy?"

What a stupid question to ask. "Obviously."

He ignores my answer and steps away to untie Harper and Levi, sliding a burger in front of each of them. "I'm sorry for tying you up, but I'm sure you've learned your lesson," he says when he gets to Levi. "Today has been stressful for all of us. We'll do something fun tomorrow. We could build something with those Legos? Play some board games?"

Now that we don't have the luxury of internet or TV, those options sound incredibly boring, as awful as that might sound. My go-to offline activity was always reading, but even that's been stripped away from me. At least curling up with a book meant I got to get lost in an alternate reality. I long for that experience now; a warm blanket draped over my lap, snuggled in my own bed, toes curling at the twists in thrillers, pulse pounding as the protagonist barely escapes the killer. Heart soaring when the romance has a happy ending. Nodding off to sleep but needing to read *just one more* chapter. Comparing book experiences with Cara over lunch and adding more books to my TBR. Nothing puts me at ease quite as much as reading, and until I get out of here, it's another loss I'll have to mourn.

Homesickness consumes my entire being, and my head sinks into my hands. Mom must be hysterical right now. She'll blame herself, and she won't sleep for days. I wonder what she's doing right now, if she's combing through the woods searching for us or sobbing in her big empty house, listening to police officers tell her they're doing everything they can to find us. This morning couldn't have been the last time I'll ever see my mother. If I'd known what awaited us today, I'd have hugged her tighter, appreciated her more.

Dad kisses each of us goodnight, promises to see us first thing tomorrow morning, then goes right back upstairs. A breeze whistles through the hole in the window, and Dad's right; the room has gotten cold, almost unbearably so. If we can't use the window to escape, we'll have to find something else.

Another idea begins to take shape. As much as I don't want to do this, I'll have to find something sharp to hit him with. Next time he brings food down, I could plunge a fork into his side, or sharpen something in this basement, then we'll make a run for it. I won't kill him, but I'll hurt him enough that he's too weak to go after us. Besides, what would he be able to do about it; call the police? He can't.

I don't want to hurt my own father. But I have to remember he hurt us first.

FOR IMMEDIATE RELEASE
JUNE 30, 2024

Local YouTube Stars Abducted by Father from Home at Gunpoint

SAWYER, ON—Police are urging anyone with information to come forward after three children were abducted by their father from their Sawyer home at gunpoint earlier this afternoon.

Doorbell footage captured at the Tower Drive residence at 3:47pm EST shows the three children—17-year-old Alyssa Bennett, 11-year-old Harper Bennett, and 7-year-old Levi Bennett, stars of the popular YouTube vlogging channel TheBennettFam—being forced at gunpoint to a waiting vehicle by father Daniel Bennett, 35, of Toronto. Police issued a province-wide Amber Alert just after 5pm today as the desperate search for the children began. There is concern for the children's safety.

The suspect, 35, male, is described as 5'11, 185lbs, with dark hair, and was last seen wearing a black hoodie with a Carhartt logo down the left sleeve, blue jeans, and a grey Toronto Blue Jays ballcap. He was seen driving out of Tower Drive with the children in a black 2021 BMW X6 with Ontario license plate DB1019.

Alyssa Bennett, 17, female, is described as 5'4, 125lbs, with long brunette hair, and was last seen wearing a white v-neck t-shirt with light blue cutoff denim shorts, and white Nike sneakers.

Harper Bennett, 11, female, is described as 4'11, 75lbs, with long brunette hair, and was last seen wearing a dark blue jumpsuit with white flowers and flip flops.

Levi Bennett, 7, male, is described as 3'9, 50lbs, with short blond hair, and was last seen wearing a plain black t-shirt and khaki shorts.

The direction the suspect travelled outside Sawyer remains unknown. This is an isolated incident and at this time, there is no threat to the general public.

If you have any information on the whereabouts of the Bennett children, please contact the Sawyer Regional Police Department immediately.

PRESS RELEASE COMMENTS:

User579242524308: *OMG!!! Who would do this to their own kids? Hope they catch that sick bastard!*
BarbieGirl345: *I always knew there was something weird about that family.*
sawyerlocal: *Praying for those sweet children and their safe return. What a betrayal from their father. I hope he doesn't harm them.*
User434953016949: *How awful! I really hope these poor kids are found safe and sound!*
GagneFarah: *Wonder if this is some kind of publicity stunt. Wouldn't be surprised.*

CHAPTER 9

I hardly sleep at all, and when I do, I dream of Mom.

She's got a flashlight in her hand, and she's all alone in the woods, bathed in the glow of the moonlight. She yells each of our names over and over, yanking branches out of her path, pulling back bushes, searching for places we might be hiding. Or—and it's something she doesn't want to think about—she's searching for our bodies. Our dead bodies.

Harper, Levi and I are each tied to a tree, our wrists bound tightly behind our backs, just like we were in the basement mere hours ago. I'd scream, but a thick layer of duct tape holds my mouth shut. Dad left us for dead, and he's hoping Mom will find us when it's too late so he can punish her for invading our privacy.

Just as she's about to reach me and save my life, I startle awake.

The basement is pitch black, and my body is stiff from the cold. I shiver under the blanket, pulling it closer to my chin. Mosquitos buzz near my head; maybe leaving a hole in the window wasn't the best idea. Next to me, Harper snores softly, and Levi faces toward me, clutching Snuggles to his chest. I wonder what they're dreaming about; if they're having nightmares like me. They almost look…peaceful, considering where we are. I release a sigh. They're counting on me, and I'm going to do everything in my power to make sure they stay safe.

The next time I wake up, streaks of golden sunlight are pouring into the room. Levi stirs, and then his eyes frantically dart around as if he's forgotten where he is. He dissolves into tears and holds Snuggles tighter before noticing I'm awake. "I want Mom," he hiccups.

I swallow my own tears. I want her, too; so badly my lungs feel as if they'll cave any minute. But I need to be brave. "I know, buddy. I promise I'm trying to get us out of here."

"When can we leave?"

"That's what I'm trying to figure out."

As if he's heard me, the basement door opens, and Dad descends down the stairs with breakfast. My heart gallops. If he's brought down sharp utensils, this could be our chance to escape. Imagining stabbing Dad makes my gut twist. They make it seem so easy in books and movies; maybe if this was a total stranger, I wouldn't be psyching myself out so much, but this is my *dad*. The man who held my grubby hands as I took my first steps. The man who taught me how to ride a bike. The man who kissed the scrapes on my knees better. The man who, up until yesterday, kept me safe. He may have said some nasty things to me in the past, but does that really outweigh all the good he's done for me?

The memory of staring down the barrel of his gun returns to me, shoving all the happy memories aside. I don't know what to do.

When he hands the plate to me—scrambled eggs, toast, and bacon—I notice a plastic fork and knife. *Dammit*. Even if I wanted to stab my own father, I couldn't. Not enough to hurt, anyway.

He greets us with a "Good morning, guys. Sleep well?" Harper finally wakes up at the sound of his voice, and she scowls. None of us answer him.

"I made you breakfast," he tries. "I'm sure you're hungry."

I push the scrambled eggs around my plate with the fork, avoiding his gaze. The smell makes my mouth water, and I take a few small bites to hold myself back from scarfing the whole plate down. I'm starving, like I haven't eaten in years.

"What do you guys want to do today?" Dad pulls one of the tote boxes out of the furnace room and sifts through it, pulling out a few board games. "We could play a game? Or like I said yesterday, we can build something with those Legos. All up to you."

"I want to play outside," says Levi.

Dad makes a face. "Not today, little man. I know it's a nice day out, but we need to stay in here just a little longer."

"But I wanna go swimming."

"We didn't even get to bring our swimsuits, Levi," Harper snaps. "And how are we supposed to go swimming when we're stuck—"

"Enough, Harper," Dad warns. "There are plenty of things for us to do in here. We can play hide-and-seek. Draw some pictures. Build a fort. You know, things people did before they had internet."

"Kids also played outside before they had internet," I add. "Adults are always begging us to go outside."

"Well, I'm the adult, and today I'm telling you you're not allowed to go outside."

Today looks like the kind of day I'd want to spend outside. There's not a single cloud in the sky, and I can tell it's *hot*. Birds chirp in the distance. It's the first official day of summer break, and if I were at home, I'd probably be swimming in our in-ground pool, wearing a new swimsuit one of our sponsors sent me, or lying on our patio, tanning and finishing the last couple chapters of *The Silent Patient*. I'd probably join Cara at the beach in the afternoon for a picnic, something we wanted to do more of this year. Mom would be barbequing something for dinner, and we'd finish off the day filming extra content for the first installment of the Bennett Summer Series on our channel. I might not get to do any of that today, but I promise myself that within a few days, I'll make it a reality.

Dad swats away a mosquito, then another, until finally he gets fed up and announces, "I'm going upstairs to see if I can find something to cover that window. The mosquitos must have come in through that hole last night. You all were probably eaten alive."

He's right; red, itchy bumps cover my skin, especially along my legs. I nod along. "Yeah, they were bad. I didn't think they'd be able to get through."

When he's gone, Harper stands and fans herself with her empty plate. "It's *way* too hot down here," she complains. "How were we freezing last night?"

"I don't know, but I'm sure we won't have to deal with it for much longer. I'm still figuring out a way to escape."

"Do you think we've been reported missing yet?"

I laugh. "Duh. Any case involving missing kids is going to be all over the news. I bet an Amber Alert was sent out. Mom has a doorbell camera, so everyone will know it was Dad who took us."

"I used to get so mad when those Amber Alerts would wake us up in the middle of the night." Harper frowns. "*Shit*, I hope other people aren't annoyed by ours. What if everyone is ignoring it because they don't think dads can kidnap their own kids?"

"Stop swearing." I sigh. "And some people probably are, to be honest. But that doesn't matter, because I bet our subscribers are raising hell all over the internet. Mom, too."

"Would she have an idea where we are?"

"I don't know. But maybe she'll remember our old cottage and come out here to look?"

Harper opens her mouth to respond, but Dad returns, and he's holding a small piece of plywood in his hands. "This should do the trick," he announces. He slips it in front of the window, and it fits like a glove. "We don't have much of these lying around upstairs, so I had to cut it to make sure it would fit. You're welcome."

"Thank you," we all echo, because that's what we're supposed to do. Thank him because he's *so* brave and always has our safety at the front of his mind. Such a hero. Dad of the year.

He grabs the scattered Legos, and convinces Levi to help him build some sort of tower. While they're doing that, I find myself staring at that pathetic piece of plywood. Not only is it blocking all the natural light, but it has also cut us off from the last bit of normalcy in our lives: seeing nature. Of course, we can take the plywood off during the day, but at night, it's going to be darker than ever down here without the moon and the stars. Man, how did I manage to take a giant rock in space for granted?

Blue skies. Green grass. Sunrises and sunsets. Rain. I can't believe I didn't appreciate these things more.

Then I get an idea.

CHAPTER 10
LAST YEAR

As usual, I've stayed up far past my bedtime to get this essay done, and I type the final words just as the clock strikes one in the morning.

My eyes burn with exhaustion, and the glow of my laptop screen prevents me from nodding off. My own half-assed words stare back at me. In this week's English assignment, I had to take on the impossible task of comparing the theme of *Hamlet* with another book I've read this year, and though Mrs. Rogers will never know, I sprinkled in some made-up scenarios. I purposely selected a book that's not popular, a book I know she'll never read. I'm not much of a writer, but I like to think it sounds pretty convincing.

Last task before bed: print out the essay and tuck it away in a nice folder.

I have to head all the way down to our home office in the basement to use the family desktop; the printer in my room fought for so long, but decided to lay itself to rest last week. I email myself the document and push the blanket off my feet as I get up, wincing at the cold. Mom and Dad are asleep just down the hall, unaware I'm still awake, so I tiptoe past their door and feel around for the stairs in the dark. If they knew I stayed up this late on a school night, they'd probably ground me. Whatever; at least it's not because I was at a party. You need a group of friends for that.

When I get to the office, I flip on the light and throw myself into the stiff pink office chair, sinking my toes into the plush carpet. Our housekeeper, Greta, left a Post-it Note next to the keyboard with the words *Have a great day!* scribbled with black marker across it. I notice the light is flashing on the computer—someone left it on—and when I move the mouse, the screen lights up to reveal a Facebook tab open in the bottom corner. Usually it's Mom forgetting to log out of her accounts, but upon further investigation, I see that it's Dad's account this time.

I need to be nosy. Bedtime can wait a little longer.

He has a few unopened notifications on Messenger. One is from a guy responding to Dad's inquiry on Marketplace for his BMW rims, and the other is from some guy named Pete Bucknell. Probably one of Dad's coworkers. Pete's message says, *Keep your head up, you'll figure it out.*

I scroll up in the conversation, and that's precisely when my world turns upside down.

Dad's message starts off with, *Hey, just wanted to say thanks for the conversation earlier. I'm sure it's not every day someone decides to dump all their family problems on you lol. I just need to get out of here.*

Pete: *All good, man, I know what that's like. Here for u anytime.*

Dad: *Thanks. I hope you don't think I'm a bad person for saying I regret having kids?*

My spine stiffens. What the hell?

Pete: *No not at all. Everyone I've ever met that had kids as a teenager basically has the same opinion. Plus ur wife putting them on the internet and all, that's gotta be tough.*

Dad: *Yeah Mel's obsession with YT is getting out of hand. Hate to say I wish I didn't have kids but can't remember the last time I was actually happy. Like it was already stressful enough having a kid at 17 but I agreed to having 2 more because she wanted them. It sounds horrible, I know. But I also love my kids. It's complicated.*

The words are a punch to the gut, and I grip the arms of the chair tight, doubling over. I might throw up. Dad regrets having me. He regrets having all of us. All the times he was ever short-tempered with us come rushing back to me; it's one thing to think your dad hates you, but to have it confirmed is a whole other level of betrayal. How can he say he loves us in the same breath as saying he wishes we were never born?

I should go to bed, but I need answers. I don't think I'll be sleeping tonight, anyway.

Pete: *Hey I get it. Sometimes I feel like things would be better if I started my life over. Different job. Different wife. Different everything. My wife's infertility problems have changed us both, and not for the good.*

Dad: *Sorry to hear that.*

Pete: *It's okay. Not to sound shallow but at least you have lots of money lol. I feel like that would fix a lot of my problems.*

Dad: *I know and I'm grateful even if it doesn't sound like I am. We got really lucky. I just wish we made this kind of money doing something else. I had to pick up my oldest daughter from school the other day because her classmates were bullying her about those videos.*

Pete: *Wow that sucks.*

Dad: *It does.*

I reach Pete's final message, wishing Dad luck, and feel my lungs deflate. I can't believe what I'm reading. Dad is upstairs right now, sleeping next to Mom, pretending to love her, pretending to love us. They seem to fight more often lately, but I had no idea it was this bad. I wonder if she knows how he really feels.

I know I'll never look at him the same again.

Tears trickle down my cheeks, and I shut the computer down without printing out my assignment. Does he dread waking up to his family in the same way I dread Mom digging out her camera? A sob escapes my throat, and I cover my mouth, even though no one will hear me all the way down here. I conclude Dad must've left this conversation open on purpose so someone would discover it. He can't be that stupid, can he?

My eyes wander around the office to the bulletin board on the wall beside the desk. There's a content schedule for the week written on the calendar; tomorrow, our *Come Grocery Shopping With Us: Family of 5* video goes up. The next day: *Weekend Trip to Buffalo, NY vlog*. We'll be filming another vlog that day, showcasing our favourite recent purchases from Amazon, since they sponsored us. Dad will stomp around as Mom sets up, mumbling about how stupid this is, then he'll plaster on a fake smile as he pretends he loves the new Smart TV he purchased for his room. Filming is always chaotic, but now that I know exactly what's running through his head, cold fingers of dread climb up my body. He's almost like a stranger to me now. It seems like any day now, one of my parents will ask for a divorce, and life as we know it will change for the worst.

As I drag myself back up to my room, I decide I hate my dad.

He said it himself; we don't make him happy. So why should I love him back? Is it selfish of me to think that? Maybe. But I don't know what to do with this new information. I definitely can't tell Mom. I'll have to hold onto it for a while until I figure out how to move forward.

With that thought in my mind, I collapse into bed and cry myself to sleep.

CHAPTER 11
NOW

Dad doesn't know it yet, but he's made it a little easier for us to get out of here.

It's simple, really. When he's not down here, I'll chip away at the broken glass, then use the plywood to cover up my progress. I doubt he'll look behind the wood at any point, unless he wants to let some sunlight in. But with any luck, it'll take me less than a day to make all that glass disappear.

The Lego tower Dad and Levi are building starts to tip over, and when it crashes to the floor, the sound startles Harper; she jumps like she's heard a gunshot. Then, without warning, she begins wailing. Hysteric, ear-splitting sobs that disturb the remaining silence. Dad immediately rushes to her, whispering a string of apologies, but she frantically kicks at him, scrambling into the corner. "No! Don't touch me!" she cries. "Get away from me!"

"Harper, sweetie, I didn't mean to scare you," Dad says gently. He tries one more time to pull her in for a hug, but she swats him away.

"I want to go home! I want Mom. And don't tell me *this* is home."

Dad shakes his head. "Listen to me. I'm not doing this out of hatred for you guys. I'm doing it because I love you. I've told you this a million times already, but you don't want to hear anything I have to say. We have to stay here. We don't have much of a choice now."

Harper is crying so hard, she's gasping for air. I wonder if she's having a panic attack. "You don't love us," she manages between breaths.

A memory rushes back to me, then. Sixteen-year-old Alyssa lying in a heap on her bed, sobbing over the Facebook messages she'd just read from her father and some other guy. *Pete.* The man who's helping Dad now. *I hope you don't think I'm a bad person for saying I regret having kids.* For a long time after discovering that message, I tried to block it out, and until now, I've kept it to myself. Not even Cara knows. But I think it's finally time to come clean to Dad about what I discovered over a year ago.

"No, you don't. You said you regret having us." I push my half-eaten breakfast away from me and look him in the eyes. My heart thumps erratically. "You can deny it all you want, but you left a chat window open with Pete a long time ago. On Facebook Messenger, right before the divorce. I read the whole thing."

His eyes darken, and I shrink down further. There's something about confronting him that still makes me uneasy, especially after everything he's done in the last twenty-four hours. My trembling hands stay in front of me in case he decides to hit me.

Harper releases another wail. "You really said that, Dad? Oh my God!"

He shakes his head. "Lissy, I didn't know you read that. I—"

"What did you mean by it?"

He clears his throat. "I don't regret you three. I meant that I regret bringing you into a world in which we failed to protect you. Your mother and I were just kids when we had you. We didn't know what we were doing. But then the whole YouTube thing started, and your mother always wanted a big family, so since we had the money, we thought that meant we were more mature. So we had more kids. Our channel just kept blowing up, so we thought we were doing something right."

"Did you have Harper and Levi for views?"

His eyebrows shoot up. "No. God, no. We'd never do that."

I consider this for a moment. "You also said you wish you could start your life over and have a different wife and different kids. Honestly, I don't feel like you're really protecting us from anything. I feel like you're only doing this for revenge."

"You have it wrong, Lissy."

"Do I, though?" I challenge. My eyes start to sting, but I blink the sensation away. I can't let him see me cry. "Your plan is to keep us imprisoned for God knows how long, and the only explanation you're offering is that it's 'for the best,' whatever that means. You don't care about how we feel; it seems like you only care about how terrible you're going to make Mom feel."

For a few minutes, he doesn't say anything, just stares up at the plywood above my head. I hope my words have punched him in the gut, made him realize how wrong this is, made him realize the best thing to do is turn himself in. But then his face reddens. "You should be thanking me," he says through gritted teeth. "I'm surprised that, even though I know you've always hated vlogging, you care this much about your mom. Suddenly you seem grateful for everything she's done for you, even though you were such a brat. Why can't you be grateful for what *I've* done for you? I sacrificed my entire life for this. Disappeared from the face of the earth. Nothing will be the same ever again. Nice to see you haven't changed."

His words strike me like a bullet. It's complicated; I'll forever be remorseful that it took me so long to appreciate Mom, but at the same time, he's right because I despised vlogging with every fibre of my being. "There wasn't an easier way to do this?" I say. "If you want to 'protect' us, all because of one stupid video Mom posted, holding us hostage is a little extreme."

"Well, then, let me show you something." He digs his phone out of his jeans pocket and begins scrolling. From afar, I can see TheBennettFam channel glaring on his screen. He clicks on an older video and holds the phone out to me. Baby Levi in a hospital bed fills the screen.

"Remember this?" Dad says.

"That's me!" Levi pipes up.

I do remember it. The video, titled "SOMETHING IS WRONG WITH OUR BABY" has over nine million views, and was recorded when Levi was only three months old. It's a three-video series documenting his two-day hospital stay as the doctors tried to figure out what was wrong with him. It was one of the scariest moments of our lives; the doctors thought there was a chance he had cancer. What kind, I can't remember. The sound of Mom's sobs returns to me now as I'm brought back to that tiny hospital room, the smell of sanitizer stinging my nostrils, the sinking feeling in my gut, the sight of my baby brother's sickly face, the nurses warning Mom she couldn't film in here. It was a little under seven years ago, but feels like it was yesterday.

Harper swipes at her eyes. "What about it? That was forever ago."

"I remember," I tell him.

Dad skips to halfway through the video. Mom is sitting in the hallway on the floor, her eyes shining. "I have some bad news, and I'm so terrified I feel sick," says Mom, her voice wobbling. "Levi is gone for some tests right now, and…they're worried about his blood counts. They think it might be leukemia, but they just want to confirm things before making an official diagnosis. I don't know what to do. I can't believe this is happening." She's shaking her head, and her speech is so quick it's almost difficult to understand. "How can my baby have cancer? He's so young. He doesn't deserve this. Please, if you could, leave some prayers for us in the comments. We need all the help we can get."

Dad looks at us expectantly. "You heard all that, right?" he says. "Well, here's the truth. He had RSV. We knew that from the beginning. At no point in time did any doctor suspect Levi had cancer. He wasn't even gone for tests in this clip; she was sitting right outside his room. But we were in debt, and she was getting desperate. And obviously, more views equals more money in our pockets."

The wind is knocked right out of my lungs. *What?*

That can't be true. She's not that much of a monster.

But why doesn't this surprise me very much?

There was controversy surrounding this series, from what I remember. Comments begging Mom to put the camera down, to spend real time with her dying baby instead of living life through a lens. Criticizing her for monetizing the videos. Criticizing Dad for not seeming concerned enough. Criticizing them for turning their baby's hospital stay into a series, like it was some form of entertainment. Even criticizing Mom for lying.

At the time, ten-year-old me thought those commenters were crazy. Mom just wanted to share their story. And she'd never lie about something so serious. After all, Levi *was* in the hospital, which was pretty hard to fake.

But the pieces are slowly coming together now as I realize this is nothing Mom hasn't done before. We've pretended to have our house broken into. We've pretended our house is haunted. We've staged countless pranks. A car cut us off in traffic a few years ago, and we made a video with the ridiculous title of "CAR ACCIDENT CLOSE CALL! *scary*". Would she really stoop so low as to pretend her child was dying?

Maybe.

"But Mom said I was a miracle baby," Levi proclaims. "So I'm not?"

"Not in the way you think, buddy," Dad says as he pats Levi on the back. "RSV is tough on babies, so sometimes it feels like a miracle that you pulled through. But you weren't dying of a terminal illness."

"What's terminal?"

"If this is true, why did you let her?" I ask, cutting off Levi. "You knew it wasn't right, but you let her film and post a whole three-video series. You're just as bad as her for not stopping it."

"You're a terrible father and I hate you!" Harper screams. "None of this would've happened if you—"

Without warning, Dad reaches across and slaps Harper's cheek with incredible force, sending her tumbling back down to the floor. She holds her face with both hands and curls into a ball, but startlingly, doesn't make a sound, though her chest heaves. It stuns us into silence.

"Now you listen to me." Dad's tone is cold. "Just because the circumstances are different does not mean *any* of you are allowed to disrespect me. Do I make myself clear?"

Harper, Levi and I exchange wide-eyed, panicked glances, but neither of us say a word. The air conditioner hums behind us.

"I said, *do I make myself clear?*" Dad says through gritted teeth, and we all nod in unison. Harper sniffles, and finally the tears begin streaming down her cheeks. I take note that he doesn't apologize to her.

"You're right; I should've stopped her but I didn't," Dad continues, scooping up a Lego piece and rolling it between his palms. "And it was wrong. We really did need the money, and that's why I didn't stop her. It makes me sick to think about. It kept me up at night for years. I thought it was the only time we'd lie for views, but I was wrong. Her last video about me is proof enough that it hasn't stopped."

I don't remember my parents ever acting so immature, but then again, when you're a kid, it seems like your parents know everything. You learn so much from them; how to sing the alphabet, how to share with your siblings, don't talk to strangers, say sorry when you hurt someone. Two smart people with jobs and so many other responsibilities surely couldn't fail, right? But here they are now, pointing the finger at each other like they're children, refusing to take the blame. I'm realizing now that they have no idea what they're doing, and never have.

Not a single apology is spoken as Dad rambles on; how can he consider this taking accountability? "When you're trying to get famous on the internet, you have to make people feel connected to you, like they know you in real life. And it was especially important for us to show the bad things sometimes because it was something they could relate to."

"Even if the bad things were made up?" I ask.

"Even if the bad things were made up."

"That's disgusting."

"I know."

With this ounce of truth revealed, it only makes the desperation to get out of here weigh heavier in my chest. When we escape, I promise myself I'll never visit him in jail, even if he writes me manipulative letters convincing me to forgive him. I steal another glance at the plywood sealing us off from the world. *Soon*, I think.

FORUM DISCUSSION

This forum was created by TheBennettFam fans for the purpose of planning search parties for the missing YouTube stars Alyssa, Harper and Levi Bennett. The police are already organizing some, but we want to help as much as we can. Please keep your comments respectful, and anyone who engages in rude behaviour will be removed immediately. We've spoken with Melissa Bennett, and she will be monitoring this forum and following up with leads. If you've found anything in your search or you know something about their disappearance, contact the Sawyer Regional Police Department immediately. Thank you everyone. Let's bring the Bennett Children home!!

Suez365: *Search party is already taking place today, July 1, 2024, by the wooded area off 5th Avenue in Sawyer, Ontario starting at 1pm. We'll be meeting up and driving out of town in any direction we're assigned. Anyone who can make it, PLEASE do. They will be covering most of the town as well. If you can't make it, no worries. Let's start organizing search parties out of town, ANYWHERE in Ontario. Dan most likely isn't keeping them in Sawyer, so we need to spread out. Anyone have theories as to where he could have taken them?*
User000014523: *I don't think he would've taken them to any big cities. Too much risk of being spotted. I wouldn't suggest searching anywhere in the Toronto area, Ottawa, Hamilton, or London. We should be focusing our attention around smaller towns. He probably took them somewhere remote.*
JohnsonJr5445: *But what if they've left the country somehow?*
Suez365: *@JohnsonJr5445 Unlikely in my opinion, as that seems too risky. He would've had to smuggle them across the border. I'm looking through their old videos right now to see if there's a location they used to visit often, since that could be a clue.*

KardashianFan: *They visited Niagara Falls recently, didn't they?*

Bookluvr: *@KardashianFan ya but that's also a big city and with lots of tourists idk if he'd go there.*

User000014523*: Northern Ontario is really remote and has tons of small towns spaced out throughout. What if we start there? Like Thunder Bay area?*

User12345678: *Who wants to do one in Wawa tomorrow? Anyone else from around there in this forum?*

PeteBucknell: *Hey everyone, Dan's coworker here. I'm about to talk to the police about it, but wanted to drop it in this chat first. A while ago, he mentioned wanting to move to Mexico, and said he wanted his kids to come with him but knew it'd be too hard to co-parent. Might be where he is now? It's not completely out of the question.*

Suez365: *@PeteBucknell OMG! Please report that asap, this information could save those kids' lives! Does Melissa know?*

PeteBucknell: *@Suez365 No, she doesn't. Tried reaching her on Instagram and am just waiting for a response. Do you have her contact info in the meantime?*

Suez365: *@PeteBucknell PMing you now.*

CHAPTER 12

Later in the afternoon, Harper, Levi and I get some alone time, so I don't waste it; it's time to start picking away at that glass.

I don't know how long we have, so I grab our makeshift ladder—the empty Lego box—and drag it under the window the second the door snaps shut behind Dad. I steady myself atop the box and wiggle the plywood out of its place in front of the window. "We need to get moving," I tell my siblings. "One of you, hold this plywood for me."

"Hold up, what are we doing now?" Harper asks as I hand her the wood.

"There's a small hole in this glass. I'm going to pick away at it until it's gone, and if Dad comes down, I'll block it with the plywood."

"Then what? What if you can't fit through the window?"

"I have another idea." I press on the glass near the hole and the cracks expand, reaching toward the corners. "Tonight, when Dad's asleep and I'm done breaking this glass, I'm going to send you and Levi through the window. You'll go to the front door of the cottage, which is probably locked, but you need to try it anyway. If it's locked, see if any of the front windows are unlocked. If they are, crawl through them and unlock this basement door. After that, we find Dad's car keys and leave in the BMW. Go straight to the closest gas station or convenience store and get them to call the police."

Harper grins, and her hands fly to her mouth. "Sometimes I don't give you enough credit. That's, like, the smartest idea you've come up with today."

I snort. "Someone had to do it."

"But what if the front windows are locked, too? Then what?"

"Then I try and fit through the window, too. It's risky, but we have to do it."

The first chunk of glass comes off in my hands with a quiet snap, and the relief makes my knees weaken. *I can do this.* I clutch it like it's a trophy, like I've sprinted the 200-meter dash in track and field and won first place. I apply more pressure to the window, taking extra precaution to ensure I don't end up needing stitches, and another piece of glass releases, landing on the window's ledge. I need a place to hide all this glass to make sure my siblings don't get hurt on the way out, and so Dad doesn't see my progress. "Levi, bring that empty tote box to me, please," I order. "I'm going to put all these pieces in there."

He deposits the blue box near my feet. "Thank you," I say. "We don't want Dad seeing these. Are there padded gloves anywhere? I don't want to cut myself."

Harper and Levi both take off to the furnace room, and the sound of tote boxes scraping across the concrete floor pierces my ears. While they search, I continue my work. The hole is big enough now that the smell of wet grass from yesterday's storm wafts inside, and I relish in it, dreaming of the moment we'll get to sink our toes into it. We're like flowers who've been cut off from the sun, starved of our essentials. If I get this right, we only have to wait a handful of hours before we'll be homeward bound.

I'm coming, Mom.

Harper's footsteps sound next to me. "We can't find any," she announces. "So be careful. We can't afford for you to bleed out."

I laugh for probably the first time since we arrived here. "Believe me, I know. We need to be able to live to exploit our story on the internet for money."

"Then we live happily ever after?"

"Yup."

"What if we run into bears tonight?" Levi asks. "Are they gonna eat us?"

"They shouldn't if we don't bother them." Another tiny shard breaks off, pricking my skin. I wince. "And if my plan goes right, we'll only have to be in the yard for a couple minutes. We shouldn't need to go through the forest."

"But what if we have to?"

"Then we have to. It's better than staying in here."

I take a step down and carefully lay some of the broken glass into the tote box. I wish I could drop them into the box from my height, but Dad might hear the impact and come down to investigate. I can't have him suspect anything. I also need to make sure I don't somehow shatter the whole window at once; again, Dad will surely hear that.

I continue to chip away at it, and soon I can stick my whole arm through the hole. Warm sunlight graces my arm, but before I can enjoy it too long, I pull it back in, praying Dad isn't looking outside. Above us, the floor squeaks with his footsteps, pacing back and forth, back and forth. I don't know what he's doing up there, but damn, that sound is like nails on a chalkboard. Stressing about something, I presume. I can't say I blame him, but at the same time, what did he expect? That Mom would just shrug it off? That our town and all our fans would magically be okay with us disappearing? He has no one to blame but himself, and I don't feel an ounce of sympathy for him.

I wonder how everyone is handling the news of our kidnapping. My classmates are probably sticking their noses right in this drama, pretending to care, pretending to have been my friend all along. I hate that this thought crosses my mind, but it does. Our fans are losing their shit online, but at the end of the day, that's a good thing; that means the news coverage will be phenomenal. Sawyer is a small town, so our residents are probably shocked that a "great family man" like my father would do something so callous. He's the villain in everyone's minds, and quite possibly the only person who doesn't hate his guts is this mysterious Pete.

Peter Bucknell. The guy who owns this dingy cottage. The guy who's helping Dad get groceries and other necessities. The guy Dad confessed his hatred toward our family to.

There has to be more to his story. He's officially an accessory to his coworker's crime; why would he be willing to put his future at risk like this?

The floor squeaks above my head again, and this time, the footsteps head toward the basement door. I act quickly. "Harper, give me that plywood right now," I say, my voice rising with each word. "Dad's coming."

Harper's face pales, but she doesn't hesitate; she thrusts the plywood at me, and I quickly shove it into its place. I don't have time to grab the leftover glass shards, so I leave them tucked behind. The game *Operation* is lying open nearby, and I order my siblings to come sit near it. "Pretend we're playing," I whisper.

The door bursts open, and Dad comes rushing down the stairs in a panic.

"Get to the car," he demands. "We have to leave right now!"

No. This can't happen. I didn't do all this planning for nothing.

"What? Why?" I rise to my feet so quickly that stars swim in my vision. "You were dead set on keeping us here."

"We can't stay here anymore." Dad is panting, and he grips the corner of the wall. "There's an Amber Alert out, and the police released doorbell footage of me. *Shit.* No one told me your mom had a doorbell camera! And traffic cameras caught my car close to the intersection where we turned on this road. If we don't get out of here right now, they might find us."

A faint glimmer of hope shines into this musty basement, and my heart hammers away in my chest. The cops are getting closer. It's both good and bad.

I never imagined I'd be begging Dad to let us stay here after the fight I've put up, but I don't have a choice. We can't leave. I need to follow through with my plan. I might not even need to if the cops find us before nighttime.

"Dad, you're panicking. Sit down." I guide him toward one of the mattresses. His forehead shines with sweat. "If you take us anywhere else, those traffic cameras will be able to find you. You'll be making the situation a hundred times worse."

He eyes me suspiciously. "I might have to take that risk. And I thought you wanted more than anything to get out of here?"

He's right. My chest tightens. "Um, well if the cops catch you on the road with us, it could put our lives in danger. The cops will try to stop your car, and if you don't willingly pull over, they'll try and cause an accident. What if that accident hurts any of us? You'll never be able to live with yourself."

"Well if we go now, we might be able to avoid a high-speed chase."

"But you said yourself the cops saw you near our closest intersection. Don't you think they're going to be monitoring that area like crazy right now?"

He sighs heavily, and his head falls into his hands. He says nothing.

I hold my head a little higher; I think it's working. "Plus, you don't have a plan for where you'd take us next, do you? You'd just drive around, wasting all that time, trying to figure something out?"

"What if I do know, and I'm just not telling you?"

"You don't. Because we would've gone there first."

He shakes his head. "You can think whatever you want. And you can hate me all you want, but at the end of the day, I know what's best for you. You're just a child."

It's supposed to be a dig at me, but instead, I let the words roll off my shoulder. I *am* still a child, but not in the way he wants. He wants me to be weak, helpless, needy. Dependent on him. Blind without his guidance. But of all the times he's pushed me down, made me feel small, this is the first time I'm going to stand right back up. One thing's for sure; I'm not going down without a fight.

"Well, *I* know what's best for me, and that involves you being in handcuffs."

He looks up sharply. "What did I say earlier about you three disrespecting me? Clearly you don't listen."

"What are you going to do about it? Ground us? Tie us up again?"

"Shut up, Alyssa. I don't know when you became such a cold-hearted bitch, but you're starting to sound just like your mother. Maybe that's why you have no friends at school."

The words strike me like a knife to the chest. I guess he never truly cared about me being bullied. Whatever. I don't need him, or anyone. I shake my head in disgust and force down the lump in my throat. He takes it as his cue to go back upstairs, but regardless of the wounds he's left me with, I've still won. He's not taking us anywhere else.

His eyes flash with warning as he retreats back up the stairs. "And remember, guys. You might think you're invincible down here, but I'm the one in control. I'm the one with the gun."

When the door closes behind him, I smirk and resume my work. That man is always contradicting himself. I hold one of the glass shards in front of me, and sunlight reflects off the corners. If our escape doesn't go as planned tonight, these would make some pretty good weapons.

CHAPTER 13
LAST YEAR

When I pull open the door of Mom's white Mercedes, her prized vlog camera is already pointed at me. "Alyssa! How was school?"

I toss my backpack into the back seat and close the door gently. Mom is always on my case about "slamming" the door, but I'm certain I've never slammed it once. "It was fine."

"Just 'fine?' Nothing interesting happened?"

"Not really."

Well, if you don't count having to face everyone again after the cafeteria incident with Laurel and Jessica. Their whole group snickered at me as I walked by, and part of me wondered if I should eat my lunch in a bathroom stall like lonely kids do. I couldn't bear to make eye contact with Blake for even a second. But aside from that, school was fine. I don't feel like talking about it.

Mom and Dad fought about that day in the cafeteria, which they seem to do a lot lately. They'll find any reason to argue these days. Dad left his socks on the floor? Mom forgot to lock her car last night? Dad answered Mom's text five minutes too late? Cue the yelling and never-ending accusations. But that day, Dad's rage was unlike anything I'd seen before. He shoved a few plates to the kitchen floor, shouting over the noise that Mom had crossed a line, then left her to sweep up the broken glass. She didn't try to defend herself this time.

Has it stopped the vlogging? No, but I wish it did. I wish I could talk about my day with *just* Mom, without millions of people listening, telling me I'm doing something wrong. Is that too much to ask?

Mom sets her camera on the dash mount and pulls out of the school parking lot. "We're headed to pick up Harper and Levi now," she tells the lens. "Harper has hockey practice later, so we're going to go home and get ready for that. Her team lost the last game, so they're really hoping they can pull ahead this time. Dad's working late tonight, so

Miss Alyssa and Levi will be coming with me. It's definitely getting busy in the Bennett household!"

I don't know if I'm supposed to say something, so I just nod along. If Mom is bothered by it, she doesn't show it.

"Levi's next hockey game isn't until tomorrow night, but I'm thinking I'll need to do some shopping in the meantime for new gear. My boy is growing up so fast, and things aren't fitting him anymore! Where did the time go?"

I stare out the window as Mom tells our viewers every detail of our day-to-day lives. Do people really care this much about us? I guess so. I shut out her voice and observe all the sights of our sleepy town as we head toward the elementary school; the naked trees swaying in the wind, people shoveling snow out of their driveways, my classmates cluttering the sidewalk as they walk home. The sky is gloomy, threatening more snow. Our viewers are often surprised we're still in Canada and not Los Angeles, but Mom and Dad both like the snow. Sometimes, it makes me wonder if they're insane; who actually *likes* this shit?

When we pull into the elementary school parking lot a few minutes later, Harper and Levi are already outside, waiting at the front doors. Mom grabs her camera and points it at them as they walk toward the Mercedes. It's not until they're close that I notice Harper's red-rimmed eyes and tear-streaked face.

Oh no.

A chilly breeze rushes into the car as they open the doors and crawl into the back seat. "Harper, what's wrong, honey?" Mom asks, and—you guessed it—keeps recording.

"Get that stupid camera out of my face!" Harper cries. "This is your fault!"

For the first time in ages, Mom actually shuts off the damn thing. Probably because there will be controversy if she posts a video of her kid begging her to stop. "Hey, don't go throwing accusations at me," she warns. "What are you talking about? Why are you crying?"

"Because of you." She wipes her eyes. "You posted that stupid video telling the whole world I got my period, and now they're all making fun of me."

My heart sinks. I knew this was going to happen, because it happened to me when I got mine. Mom filmed a lengthy video going over all the details, then took me shopping for pads, vlogging every second of it. She'd chime in with, "I can't believe my baby girl is growing up," and, "I'll never forget my first period!" But the one quote that really stuck with my classmates was, "You're not a girl anymore; you're a woman!" They wouldn't let that go for weeks.

When the classroom fell silent, they'd play the video on full blast for everyone to hear. They dipped tampons in red Kool-Aid and left them on my desk, on my chair, in my locker. They'd tell me I was gross. If I told them to leave me alone, they'd say I must be having PMS. It was a nightmare, and now that my little sister is going through the same thing, I suddenly feel protective of her. I want to break Mom's camera. I want something terrible to happen to every single kid bullying Harper. I want this ridiculous oversharing to end.

Mom backs out of her parking space. "Tell them to grow up. Getting your period isn't anything to be ashamed of, and those girls will eventually get theirs. Maybe they are just jealous."

"Who the heck would be jealous about a *period*?" Harper sobs.

"Insecure girls. It happens all the time."

"Well, what about the boys, then? It's mostly boys picking on me. And I want you to delete that video! It's embarrassing!"

"I'm sorry, Harper, if it made you feel that way. But you have to remember, these videos could help other girls out there. As women, we should feel empowered, not ashamed of our periods. People need to talk about it more and end the stigmas surrounding it. Do you understand, honey?"

"No, I really don't!"

My heart tugs; she's so distraught. "Mom, just delete the video," I say. "You remember what happened with my video. I was basically tortured at school."

"But they eventually forgot about it, didn't they?" Mom rests her hand on my thigh. "It's going to be okay. Deleting the video isn't going to fix the problem. I'll have a talk with the principal and tell her to do something about those kids, because the last thing I want is for any of you to be bullied."

Harper whimpers. "You care more about the money. You won't delete the video because my period is making you money."

"Excuse me?" Mom whirls around, taking her eyes off the road for a few seconds. "Don't you dare accuse me of things I didn't do. You're making me out to be the worst mother in the world, when in reality I've given you *everything*. This has nothing to do with money. Tell you what. You're grounded after tonight's game, and you're not going to Haven's birthday party anymore."

"*Mom!*"

"I'm serious, Harper. You don't get to disrespect me. That's not how this works."

Harper sobs the rest of the way home, and Levi and I remain silent; if we intervene further, we might face a similar punishment. If I had the login to our YouTube channel, I'd delete the video myself and take the fall, but right now, there's nothing I can do for her except tell her how I got through it. I'll have to have a big-sister talk with her later.

Mom's right; having your period is nothing to be ashamed of. But why is it anyone's business, anyway?

When we get home, I notice Dad's home early for once. He walks to the foyer to greet us, but Harper storms past him, running up to her bedroom and slamming the door as hard as she can. "What's her problem?" he asks, jerking his thumb in her direction.

"Oh, she's pissed about the period video," Mom scoffs. "Kids are bullying her about it."

Dad's face begins to redden. "Are you kidding me, Mel? You're giving the kids at school something to bully our kids about?"

"Go ahead, blame me like everyone else!" Mom throws her hands up. "So it's my fault now."

"It is! Listen to yourself. You don't care that they're teasing her. You needed content!"

"Well, you didn't seem to have a problem with the video before I uploaded it."

"I did. You just don't listen to me. Enough is enough with making our kids targets at school."

"Why are my videos the problem? Why aren't we blaming the kids at school for being assholes? Or their parents, for raising assholes?"

They take their argument into the kitchen, and I grab Levi by the sleeve, leading him upstairs. We don't need to listen to them fight again. "C'mon, let's go see Harper," I say.

"Are Mommy and Daddy gonna hurt each other?" he asks as he climbs the stairs.

"No, they won't," I say, and I feel a pang of guilt. They just might hurt each other, and I'm not sure who will hurt who first. I might be lying to my little brother.

NEW VIDEO FROM THEBENNETTFAM
CHAT WITH PETE BUCKNELL - BRING MY KIDS HOME!

Good morning everyone, and welcome back to the channel. Before I begin, I just want to thank you all from the bottom of my heart for your help so far in trying to bring the kids home. It means more than you'll ever know, and without all of you, I don't know what I'd do. We have so many eyes on this case, and I'm positive this means we're getting closer to finding them. So again, thank you all so, so much. I hope to find a way to repay you someday.

I also want to take some time to thank all the officers and detectives at the Sawyer Regional Police Department for their commitment to this case. They're working so incredibly hard, day and night, to find my kids, and I appreciate everything they do. They've been so quick to organize search parties and investigate every possible lead. This job can't be easy for them, but they're doing everything they can. If you have some extra time today, I'd suggest leaving them a comment on their social media accounts to thank them for everything they're doing!

Recently, some fans started a forum post to discuss possible leads, and that brings me to the topic of today's video. Through that forum, I was put in contact with Pete Bucknell, who is sitting right beside me, because he has some important information to share that may give us clues as to where the kids are. Now Pete, if you could introduce yourself to the audience, please?

Pete: Yes, hi everyone. My name is Pete Bucknell, and I'm a coworker of Dan's. We work at an accounting firm together in Toronto. I also met Mel many years back, and while we don't really know each other that well, I've always known that she is an amazing, strong, hardworking woman. Mel, I can't even begin to imagine what you're feeling right now. So I'm really hoping that the information I'm about to share helps in some way.

Melissa: *Aw, thank you so much, Pete. It really means so much to me.*

Pete: *Any time, dear.*

Melissa: *So, let's talk about what brings you here today, Pete. You mentioned a few things in the forum that really caught my eye. And since you know Dan personally, I imagine you could probably provide some insights as to how he's been acting for the last little while. Let's start with what you know.*

Pete: *Okay. Well, the day Dan kidnapped the kids, he suddenly quit his job at our accounting firm, without giving a two-week notice or a reason, really, as to why he was quitting. He just showed up that morning, said it would be his last day, then he left. To put things into perspective, he's been working at this accounting firm for as long as I have, which is thirteen years. It seemed strange.*

Melissa: *Yes, and when we were together, he always talked about how much he loved that job. That does seem really strange for him to do that.*

Pete: *For sure. Not long before that, like I mentioned in the forum, Dan had a conversation with me about how he wished he could move to Mexico. He raved about the weather, the beaches...just about everything. But he said the only thing holding him back was his kids. He wouldn't be able to co-parent while living there. He would only be able to see his kids, like, once or twice a year if he moved there, so it seemed like the obvious choice to stay in Canada. I forgot about that conversation until he took the kids. I think he took them there.*

Melissa: *Did he ever mention where in Mexico he wanted to live?*

Pete: *Unfortunately, no, he didn't.*

Melissa: *I know it sounds ridiculous to say, but did he ever hint at forcibly taking the kids there?*

Pete: *Again, no. Not that I noticed, anyway. But he would talk negatively about you a lot, so I think it's strongly related, especially considering he took your kids at gunpoint. He really didn't want you to have them.*

Melissa: *What sort of things did he say about me?*

Pete: *He claimed you were holding him back from doing what he really wanted in life, one of those things being the ability to live anywhere in the world. He talked about wanting full custody all the time. There were even times he said he wanted to get back together with you, but you didn't want that.*

Melissa: No, definitely not. We had our issues, and at the end of the day, I decided it was best for the kids if we divorced. It was so toxic for them, listening to their parents constantly fighting. I'd rather two happy households than one unhappy one.

Pete: That makes a lot of sense. And I hate to say it, but considering the last video you posted before the kidnapping was a video of you talking about the divorce, it may have been the final straw for him. I think he had so much hatred built up for you that he couldn't bear to watch you be happy anymore, so he took the kids and fled the country.

Melissa: The kids looked so terrified of him in that doorbell footage...sorry, it really chokes me up talking about it. He pointed a gun at his own children. Did you know he had a gun?

Pete: A few months ago, he left work early a few times to take a firearms course to get his license. We talked about it sometimes, since I have mine. I go hunting with some buddies occasionally, and he expressed interest in joining us. He would occasionally ask me questions about the course.

Melissa: What kinds of questions?

Pete: If I found shooting a gun easy. If I found the course easy.

Melissa: Oh, my God. What about the kids? Did he talk about them?

Pete: All the time. They were his pride and joy. He complained a lot that he hardly ever saw them. He sometimes said his family was "broken."

Melissa: So you don't think...sorry...you don't think the purpose of the gun is to hurt the kids? Do you think it's more for the purpose of hurting people who get in his way?

Pete: I think so, yes. Dan is a pretty complicated man, but I don't think he'd ever hurt them. If anything, I think he pointed the gun at the kids to scare them into doing what he wanted, which was to come with him. Without it, they might have refused to leave, since they seemed so happy with you.

Melissa: I see. If he took them to Mexico, I wonder how he would have gotten across the border. Don't they need some sort of permission slip or statement from the other parent?

Pete: I'm willing to bet he would have crossed the border illegally. How, I don't know. He was distracted a lot at work the last few months...maybe researching how to pull this off? He was very withdrawn.

Melissa: So it sounds like this took Dan months of planning, regardless of where he went. It's crazy to think that, during those months, he hardly ever called the kids or came to see them. We don't live that far from Toronto, honestly, and I've never stated he can't come see them. I was starting to think he had no interest.

Pete: No, quite the opposite, actually. I don't know why he never came to see them. He seems to want to make up for it now, though.

Melissa: I wish he would have gone about it a better way than this. I'm trying not to blame myself for this, but you're right; it happened right after I posted that video, which likely made him act on his plan, maybe even earlier than he thought. I regret that video so much, you have no idea. I would never have posted it if I thought it was going to put my kids in danger, and I'm so fucking sorry. But no matter what it takes, I'm going to find them. I will see them again. He's not going to win this time.

Pete: Don't blame yourself, Mel. At the end of the day, he's the one who committed the ultimate crime of kidnapping his own children. Justice will be served. I promise.

Melissa: Thank you so much, Pete. It really means a lot. And I'm so thankful you came forward with all that information. I think it's really going to help with this investigation, and hopefully direct the police to start some kind of search in Mexico. They told me this morning that they're looking through his work computer, so maybe they'll be able to find where he's taken them.

Pete: That's great news. I'm happy I could help in some way, and I hope everything I've told you leads to a break in this case. No mother deserves to go through what you're going through right now.

Melissa: Thank you again, Pete. Glad to have you here.

With all of the information we've just heard from Pete, I'm urging all our viewers from Mexico to keep your eyes peeled. It's a bit of a long shot, but you never know. If you see anything unusual, or think you recognize Dan or any of the kids, please don't hesitate to report it to the authorities immediately. We're offering a $5000 reward for anyone who can help point us in the right direction and find the kids.

And if you're somehow watching: Alyssa, Harper, Levi; my sweet babies. Mommy loves you all so much, more than I could ever put into words. You're my whole world, my sun, my moon, my stars. I'm so sorry for everything you're going through right now. I'll never give up searching for you, and I promise to never let something like this happen to you again. Just hang in there a little longer; Mommy's coming to get you.

COMMENTS:

User1892476: *I'm so grateful for people like Pete. Thanks so much for coming forward, and I really hope this means something! I can't even begin to imagine what those poor babies are going through right now :(*

Aquagurlll: *It gives me some comfort to know the kids are probably alive. I just hope they aren't suffering.*

MikeR: *If any of you sheep believe this shit, then the world is doomed. This is so clearly staged. Melissa will be laughing all the way to the bank after making her "it was all a prank" video!!!*

    Iluvturtles101: *@MikeR Wow, you're a piece of work. There's literally video evidence. Get off the internet and take your hatred elsewhere old man.*

    User67676767: *@MikeR A mother is missing her CHILDREN, have some sympathy. Don't you have anything better to do than spam the comment section of a woman you don't even know? Get a life.*

    MikeR: *Go ahead, keep making me laugh. I could do this all day.*

    Iluvturtles101: *@MikeR Troll.*

Penguinzz: *Thank you Pete, and thank you to the police officers for all their hard work! We WILL get Alyssa, Harper and Levi home safely <3*

CHAPTER 14

NOW

By the time Dad comes back downstairs two hours later, I've already made quite a bit of progress with my window.

I have managed to get more than half of the window open, with only a few cuts to my hands. Once Dad is back upstairs, I'll only need about an hour of uninterrupted time to clean this up the way I'd like, then we can begin our travels overnight. Bugs have started to swarm the open glass, trickling into the basement, and I'm hoping Dad won't notice how much they've multiplied. If he'd been smart about this whole kidnapping thing, he wouldn't have put us in an area with a window in the first place, but he must think we won't fit anyway. Good thing I'm about to prove him wrong.

At the sound of his approaching footsteps, I quickly slide the plywood into place, move my Lego box/ladder out of the way and drag out our half-finished game of *Connect 4*. Harper and Levi know the drill; they rush to sit in a circle with me, and Levi picks up a blue game piece, pretending to play along. I'd like to think I've staged this scene fairly well; three siblings bonding together, without the internet, perfectly safe from the world. Dad cracks a smile when he sees us. "So, who's winning?" he says cheerfully, lowering himself onto the floor next to us.

"Me," says Levi, raising his hand.

"That's awesome, buddy. You seem to be getting better at this game."

"I'm trying."

"Care to let me join next round?"

"I guess."

Dad doesn't acknowledge our earlier argument or insist we need to leave again; instead, he plasters the biggest smile he can muster onto his face, playing the role of Good Dad. It's a great way to end our remaining time in this basement, even if he's faking it. I can't have tensions escalate any further, or he might start to get suspicious and watch us more carefully. He's become incredibly unpredictable, which means I might not be finished with convincing him to keep us here. For now, I need to keep my act up for just a few more hours, maybe less if the police get here before then.

I decide to immerse myself in the game and pick up a red game piece, blocking Levi's last move. Games are just about the only thing Dad left us with down here to pass the time, and I can only play them so much before they get boring. Better than doing nothing, I guess. "Ready to lose?" I quip as Levi drops another game piece in front of mine.

"You wish!" Levi laughs.

"I always win. Don't kid yourself."

"Well then, prepare to be disappointed."

"What happened to your hand, Lissy?" Dad reaches across me and takes my hand in his, inspecting it, and that's when I realize the small trail of blood trickling down my finger, toward my palm.

I bristle. *Crap*. This cut must've reopened. How did that happen?

I take a deep breath to calm myself down. I scramble to find an excuse he'll believe. "Oh. I had a scab from helping Mom chop carrots last week. I nicked myself with the knife. I must've scratched it by accident."

He raises a brow. "That long ago, and it still hasn't healed? That seems like a lot of blood."

I gulp. "Yeah, it was pretty deep."

"Are you sure? You better not be lying to me."

"Not lying."

"I watched it happen," Harper chimes in. The urge to hug her consumes my entire being. "Mom thought it might need stitches at first, but then it stopped bleeding."

"Okay, then," Dad says slowly. "So you're one hundred percent sure your mom didn't do this to you? You can tell me if she did. I won't be mad at you."

My head snaps in his direction. "You honestly think Mom would *stab* me? Or cut me in any way? Come on. Even you know that's a bit of a stretch, considering she's never laid a hand on us."

The change in subject makes my tensed muscles relax, despite the accusations toward Mom. He clearly doesn't suspect that the cut came from my attempted escape. I'd consider that a win.

"Okay. You do need a Band-Aid, though. I'll be right back." He climbs to his feet and opens the adjacent bathroom door, then rifles through the medicine cabinet. When he returns, he instructs me to hold my hand out, and he wraps the Band-Aid around my finger nice and snug. It reminds me of being a little kid again, having Dad fix my boo-boos after falling off my bike or taking a tumble at the park, and suddenly I'm swallowing the threat of tears. For the millionth time since being kidnapped, I wonder when he changed from that loving father to *this*.

He wasn't always a great father, but he wasn't always an awful father, either. On the days when the insults were particularly bad, I'd curl up in bed and sob into my pillow, wishing I had a different dad, one who didn't call me names and berate me for small mistakes. But the next day, he'd make up for it by taking us out for ice cream, or bowling, or a road trip to our favourite waterpark. Things weren't constantly bad growing up; I was a lot more privileged than I realized. I'm trying not to let the bad memories wash out the good ones, but it hasn't been easy since we got here.

Once I'm all bandaged up, Levi wins the round, and the sound of his cheers drowns out my thoughts of the past. "See, I told you I'd win," he says smugly, sticking his tongue out at me. "How does it feel to be a loser?"

"I don't know how I'll ever get past it," I mock-cry, and he hollers with laughter. "My own little brother, crushing my dreams of becoming a *Connect 4* champion."

"We can get past it by playing another game," says Dad. "What do we want to play now?"

He gets up and starts to head toward the tote box full of games. I watch him over my shoulder and freeze when I realize which tote box he's reaching for; the one full of glass.

I left it out.

No.

My stomach twists, and I shoot to my feet at the same time as Harper shrieks, "Wait!"

The panicked edge in her voice might have ruined this for us. He spins around, his brows drawn tightly. "What?"

My heart pounds in my throat. I can't let him see what's inside the box; just thinking about his reaction to seeing the glass makes my spine tingle with fear. "That's not the box with the games," I tell him as calm as I can muster. "It's over there in the corner."

"Why is this one out here, then?" He moves closer to it, and my breath catches in my throat. "I didn't see this earlier. What's in it?"

"It's empty," I blurt before I can stop myself. "It…uh…we were using it earlier to play hide-and-seek. Levi closed himself inside it. There aren't many places to hide down here, so we got creative."

Dad seems to consider this for a moment. I will him not to move the box; the glass will make so much noise, and that will be a dead giveaway. I don't want to know what he'll do to us if he finds out about the window. "That bored, huh?" he finally says.

I nod. "Well, we were just trying to think of things to do other than play board games and build stuff with Legos. So that's what we came up with."

"I see." He scratches his head. "If you wanted other things to do, you could have just asked me, you know. You didn't have to resort to playing inside tote boxes."

"I didn't know if you had anything else. That's all."

When he steps away from the glass-filled box and kneels beside the box filled with games, I release the breath I was holding. "Anything you need, just tell me, okay? I can get things delivered here. And if I'm ever not down here with you and you need something, just knock at the door. I'll be here in a heartbeat."

My heart hasn't quite settled yet from that scare, and jolts of nervous energy ripple through my limbs. I manage another quick nod before diverting his focus back to the task at hand; finding another game. "Do you have *Guess Who?* in there? I haven't played that one in a long time."

"Yeah, I love that game," Harper chimes in, playing along. "We used to play that one all the time. Remember, Dad?"

"Of course I do." He lifts the lid off the box and removes a few games as he searches for the one we want. "Our board game nights were my favourite. You were totally obsessed with *Guess Who?* when you were little. Your face would light right up every time you got the right answer."

Harper and I both smile. Every Sunday evening after dinner, all of us would gather at the kitchen table and pick a board game to play. We dubbed it "Bennett Family Game Night." Before our channel really blew up, we hardly vlogged it at all, so it was one of the only times we spent together without a camera joining us. Movie nights, too. I can't remember when these nights stopped, but it's been years. "I miss those days," I find myself saying. And it's true; I was always able to let loose and have fun during those nights. It was basically the only day of the week we had off.

"So do I," Dad says wistfully. He finds *Guess Who?* and holds it out for all of us to see. "Bingo."

We get to work setting the game up, and sit in a circle around each other. "I think we should bring back Bennett Family Game Night," Dad adds. "Would you guys like that? Every Sunday after dinner, just like we used to."

"I'd love to," I say, and my siblings follow suit. Little does Dad know I'm playing my own game, one where I pretend to care about what he wants. I'll give him this one night to live in his fantasy world, but after this, I'm going to turn my back on him. And I'll never look back.

CHAPTER 15

The four of us become so engrossed in our games that time escapes us. Before we know it, Dad glances down at his watch and exclaims, "Oh, it's past seven! You guys are probably starving. What do you want for dinner tonight?"

Seven o'clock. I'd better get to work if I want to get us out of here tonight. "Do you have pizza?" I ask.

"Yep, a few frozen pizzas." He tucks *Guess Who?* back into its box. "You're okay with that?"

"It'll do," says Harper.

"Gotcha. I'll be right back." He pushes the tote box full of games aside, then he's gone.

Harper, Levi and I exchange glances when the door clicks shut behind him. It's like a routine now; as soon as we're alone, I remove the plywood, Harper brings me the Lego box/ladder, Levi brings me the glass-filled tote box, and I pull the glass out until my hands hurt. This time, spiders have crowded at the corners of the window and onto the plywood, and I fight the urge to gag as I work around them. Mosquitos buzz next to my ear. Golden evening sunlight pours in, and it reminds me of Mom, how "golden hour" has always been her favourite time to shoot Instagram content. An ache forms in the centre of my chest. I can't wait to get home, but at the same time, I never noticed until now that I was kind of enjoying the break from social media.

Isn't that kind of messed up? The only way we could escape the cold grip of the internet was to get kidnapped?

Hah. If I could explain this to ten-year-old Alyssa, she'd pass out.

"Holy crap, you're basically done!" Harper whisper-shrieks behind me. "I can't believe you did it."

I wiggle the glass, and another piece snaps off. I can't help but grin; Harper, ever the critic, has found it in her heart to be proud of me. My heart warms a little knowing she trusts me to keep her safe. "Yep. We'll be out of here before you know it."

"And now we just wait until it gets dark until we make our move?"

"You got it."

The rest of the job only takes ten minutes. When I yank the last remaining piece of glass out of the window, the urge to scream with joy bubbles in my chest, but I force it down, instead choosing to pump my fists in the air. I did it. Good God, I did it. We now have a perfect gap within the basement walls to escape our little prison, and it's all because of my failed attempt to break a window with a lunchbox. Some things just work out in the end.

"Oh my God," I breathe. "It worked."

We silently celebrate our victory with a group hug, then Levi breaks away to start jumping. We're not quite in the clear, though, and the thought hovers over me like a dark cloud. Dad could still peek behind the plywood at any time, so we'll have to play it safe until he goes to bed. I make a point to avoid mentioning it to my siblings so I don't kill their joy. Right now, we need something to look forward to.

I slip the plywood back in place, and we resume our spot on the floor with another game: *Snakes & Ladders*. Only a few more hours of this boring shit, then I'll get to go home and finish reading *The Silent Patient*.

***

When Dad kisses us goodnight at nine o'clock, heat floods my cheeks. I've never been so nervous for something in my life; I'd rather be humiliated in front of Blake in the cafeteria a million times over.

Breaking out of a basement. Breaking back into the house without Dad hearing to nab his keys. Stealing Dad's car and having to navigate an unfamiliar area in the dark with no GPS. It's so far out of my comfort zone it makes me sick, but I have to do this, for me, for my siblings, for Mom. There are so many ways this could go wrong, things I can't stomach thinking about right now, but for once in my life, I have to trust my own judgment here.

I won't be able to live with myself if I mess this up. I have no backup plan.

Dad shuts out the lights and closes the basement door, plunging the room in total darkness. Now we wait. I can't sleep. Won't sleep. My heart pounds an unsteady rhythm, so loud I can hear it. I'll wait a few hours, but how am I supposed to know when he's asleep? And with no watch or phone, I'll either need to count the minutes down or guess how much time has passed since he left the basement.

"Alyssa?" Levi whispers to my right. "I'm really scared."

I roll to face him. "It's going to be okay, buddy. I won't let anything happen to you."

"I don't want to go first out the window. Can Harper go first?"

"Screw that, I'm not going first!" Harper hisses. "I don't want—"

"Enough," I warn. Wow, I'm really starting to sound like Mom. "We don't have time to argue about who goes first. It can't be me, because I don't know if I'll fit. But if you want to get out of here, someone has to do it."

"Fine, but I'm still scared," Levi declares.

"You just have to be brave. You think you can do that for us?"

"Maybe. I'll try."

"Good. That's the attitude we need. I know it's scary, but as long as you try, we'll be out of here in no time."

Harper yawns. "I wish I could sleep right now, but we're going to have to pull an all-nighter, aren't we."

We definitely don't have time for sleep. Even if I wanted to, I'm too on-edge for my body to let me. "Maybe. But we don't need to worry about that right now."

"How long do we have to wait?"

"Not sure yet."

So we wait. And wait and wait and wait. I lie back on the air mattress and stare up at the ceiling, blinking away the heaviness in my eyelids. The mattress is deflating a little, and it sinks with my weight. I try to imagine what I'd be doing right now if I was at home; probably lying in bed with my laptop next to me, watching one of my favourite vloggers travel the world. Maybe reading the next book in my TBR pile. Maybe scrolling through the comments on our newest video, relishing in all the praise sent our way. I might even be sleeping, even though it's summer break and I'm usually up until at least midnight. Tomorrow, I promise myself, I'll get to do all of these things again.

I don't hear Dad's footsteps upstairs anymore, which means he must be lying in bed. It doesn't mean he's sleeping; maybe he's reading or watching a movie. I wonder if what he did to us keeps him awake at night, if that will throw a wrench into my plan.

Waiting is killing me. It's making me think too much. I hate this.

Soon enough, I hear Harper and Levi snoring softly next to me. I'll let them have their sleep; the last thing I need is two moody, sleep-deprived siblings weighing me down. I stare at the ceiling some more, then swat at a few mosquitos, then daydream/worry about our escape. *Soon.*

***

I can't take the waiting anymore; it's time to go.

I shake Harper and Levi's shoulders, and they stir. "Ready?" I ask them. "I think it's been a few hours."

Harper groans. "Already?"

Annoyance bites at me. "Yes, already. Now get up."

While I wait for them, I quietly drag the Lego box to the window and take a step up to remove the plywood. For a few minutes I just stare at my masterpiece, give myself a pat on the back. The moment we've been waiting for is finally here.

It's pitch-black outside, with no moonlight or stars to guide us. Clouds have rolled in, and I wonder if it might rain. I haven't had much practice driving in the dark, especially when it's raining, and I'd be lying if I said the thought didn't make my stomach clench. My whole body tenses as Harper and Levi approach, ready to go. It's now or never.

I step down. "Okay. Levi, I'm going to lift you up to the window first, and you're going to crawl out as carefully as you can. When you're out there, don't go anywhere; wait for Harper. I'll lift her out next, and then you'll both go around to the front of the cottage. Remember what to do after that?"

Harper nods. "We try the door to see if it's unlocked. If it isn't, we try the front window. If the window is locked, then you try to squeeze out this window."

"That's right." I wipe sweat from my forehead and pray that one of those things is unlocked. We're in the middle of nowhere, so really, there's no reason to lock them. There's a chance he did for extra precaution, though, and if that's true, then I'll want to hope I can hoist myself up to the window with no help and fit through. "Are we ready?"

"Yep, I'm ready," says Levi. He joins me on top of the Lego box, and I cradle my hands under one of his feet like I'm a cheerleader and he's my flyer. It's easier than I thought to lift him, and he grabs the ledge with all his might, pulling himself through the gap. Just like that, he's outside. He turns to give me a thumbs up before pressing himself up against the house and sinking into the grass to wait for Harper. I smile to myself; this is going easier than I thought already.

Harper sighs as she inches closer to me. "I'm scared, Alyssa," she says, her voice wobbling. "I don't know if I can do this."

"It's okay," I assure her. "If Levi did it, so can you."

"But what if it goes wrong? What if Dad wakes up and sees us? Oh my God, I can't."

Tears start to trickle down her cheeks, and she fans her eyes. While I should be comforting her, I can't help but feel a twinge of frustration. "Harper, we don't have much time to think about it. We just need to act. Please, trust me."

She sniffles. "Okay. I'm ready."

It's tougher to get her out the window since she's heavier than Levi, but I force all my strength into lifting her, and she does the rest of the work for me. Just like Levi, she grips the ledge tightly and pushes herself all the way up, crawling the rest of the way out. She barely fits, which means there's no way I will, but I push that thought aside. *Almost there.*

"Hurry," I whisper. "And be as quiet as you can. If you need to talk to each other, don't let Dad hear you."

They exchange glances, and then they're both gone, the sounds of Harper's sniffles becoming more distant. I sink down onto one of the air mattresses and suddenly let the guilt swallow me; I shouldn't have let them go out there all by themselves. They were both terrified. Was there a better plan I could've come up with to allow me to face the danger first? Should I have gone ahead and used the glass shards as weapons instead? Would I have had the courage in the first place?

No. Maybe. I don't know.

This is the better way. At least, I hope so.

It's another waiting game as I strain my ears to listen for the doorknob twisting with my siblings' arrival, my ticket to getting out. I pull my knees to my chest and hang my head, listening to the blood rush through my ears. *Please let them be okay. They're just kids. It was all my idea. Please let this work; we deserve better than this.*

Exhaustion creeps up on me again, weighing down my limbs. I can't wait for this night to be over, and can't help but wonder what life will be like after the sun rises and begins a new day. Will we still be trapped down here? Will we be home, swarmed by reporters itching to get every detail of our story? Will Mom plan to film some sort of "documentary" for our channel? Will she finally grant us the privacy we deserve?

My thoughts are interrupted by the sound of the door.

It's Harper and Levi; not Dad. Relief hits me like a hurricane. I could cry.

Before I meet them, I reach into the glass-filled tote box and snag one of the shards. I head into the bathroom and wrap it in one of the cloths, then slip it into the pocket of my shorts. I shouldn't need it, but it doesn't hurt to be prepared. I tiptoe across the concrete floor and up the rickety steps, careful to avoid the creaks, then gently close the door behind me. When Dad gets up in the morning, I want him to think we're still down there and get the surprise of his life when he finds the basement empty. "The door was locked," Harper whispers as I notice the open window to my left.

My eyes scramble to find the BMW keys in the dark. When Dad lived with us, he'd always hang his keys on a hook by the door, but I don't see one. There are two small shelves close to the door, and they also hold nothing. I carefully make my way into the nearby kitchen to check if they're on the table, but nope; empty. *Come on Dad, where the heck are your keys?*

"Did you find them?" Harper asks.

I whirl around and press a firm finger to my lips, willing her to shut up for five minutes, and her eyes widen. *Sorry*, she mouths.

Desperation climbs through me as I quietly sift through the junk cluttering the hutch. *Please don't wake up please don't wake up please don't wake up.* We're running out of time. He's hidden them well, and I wonder if that was intentional. I push some old mail to the side and check underneath, but nope; not there either. *What the hell?*

A horrible thought dawns on me. He must have them with him in the bedroom. I've looked everywhere for those keys, and I know he's not stupid enough to have left them in the car. I steal a glance down the hallway at the closed door and fight the urge to scream in frustration; there's no way I can sneak in there without him hearing me.

I hang my head in defeat. "We'll have to walk," I tell my siblings.

Harper gasps. "We can't! What if we—"

The light in Dad's bedroom flickers on.

CHAPTER 16

The blood drains from my face. *No no no no no.*

"Run!" I hiss, and Harper and Levi bolt toward the door. I follow hot on their heels just as the bedroom door swings open, and Dad emerges.

"Where the fuck do you think you're going?" he bellows, and his heavy footsteps sound behind me, closer than I'd like them to be.

Harper is the first to the door, and when it's open, the three of us take off running faster than we've ever run before. The dark, ominous woods stand before us, and as much as the sight sends a jolt of fear up my spine, I make a beeline straight toward them. "This way!" I holler.

Harper is much faster than me, thanks to all the cross-country running practice and track and field. She zips right by me, and it's so dark I almost lose her. I can't risk leaving Levi behind, so I grab hold of his arm just as a hand closes around my other wrist, yanking us both to the forest floor. I scream and let go of my brother. "Keep going!" I yell.

Levi scrambles to his feet, and Harper circles back around. "Alyssa, no!" she shrieks.

Dad pulls me into a headlock, and I squirm against his body. The crook of his elbow presses against my throat, choking me, and I gasp for air. "You think you're so clever, you little bitch," he snarls.

I claw at his arms and swing my knee right into his groin, which causes him to release a cry of pain and loosen his grip. I kick him again. "Nice try," I spit, and then I'm running again as fast as my legs can carry me. My breath comes in short bursts as I catch up to my siblings. "Hurry!" I urge, and take Levi's hand again.

Levi starts to sob. "Alyssa, he's coming to get us!"

"He won't catch us if we keep running," I assure him. I shouldn't promise him anything, but I need to keep him calm. "Watch out for the tree roots."

Branches claw at my face, and I give up on pushing them aside, instead focusing on the uneven ground below my feet. I can't see much, but there are roots everywhere, and we stumble over them a few times as we run deeper into the woods. I don't hear Dad anymore, but there's no way he's given up that easily. I don't have time to check over my shoulder to see if he's still there; all I can do is keep running.

Harper stops a few feet ahead of us, folding at the waist and gasping for air. "Is he gone?"

"I don't know, but we need to keep going." I wish I could take a break; my lungs burn, reminding me how unfit I am. Maybe I'll have to start hitting the gym once I'm home. "Don't worry about him right now."

"But what if he kills us?" Her tone becomes hysterical. "I don't want to die!"

"He's not going to—"

My words are interrupted by an ear-splitting pop noise; the unmistakable sound of a gunshot. Harper screams.

"Come out of the woods, and I won't hurt you," Dad calls out. I don't think he can see us, but we're not far enough away from him. "If you don't, well, you won't like the punishment. Because I *will* catch you."

He's bluffing. He has to be. Just earlier, he told me he never intended to use the gun on us. Now, I'm not so sure what to believe.

All I know is that we have to keep running.

I take my siblings' hands on either side of me, and together we sprint deeper into the woods. Twigs snap at our feet, and I hope they don't give away our location too much. I have no idea where we're going, but until we lose sight of him, we're not stopping.

Another shot blasts through the night air, and I hear the bullet graze the grass right next to us. *Fuck.* He's shooting at us now. If he'd aimed at a slighter angle, he would've hit one of our ankles. My stomach lurches. "Faster!" I whisper, and pump my legs harder. Harper whimpers.

"You could make it easy for all of us, you know." Dad's voice is faint now, but it still cuts deep. "Tell you what. You come back right now, and I'll strike you a deal. Stay with me for one more week, and I'll drive you back to Sawyer and drop you off at the edge of town, no questions asked."

I duck behind a tree to catch my breath, and Harper and Levi follow suit. "Under the condition that your mother quits the YouTube thing for good," he continues. "If she doesn't, well, I'll find out, and you'll come back with me. It's really that simple."

It's not a terrible deal. Part of me aches to surrender, to give him what he wants, to stop this cat-and-mouse game. The logical side of me is screaming that he's lying. But what if he's had a change of heart?

"I've realized that you're right, Lissy. Keeping you imprisoned here is no way for kids to live. I messed up; I know. If I bring you back to Sawyer, I know the chances of seeing you three again are slim." He chokes up a little. "I'll be on the run from the cops for the rest of my life. But if your mom promises to keep you safe, it'll be worth it to see you happy again. I don't want to hurt you, but if you don't come back, I won't have a choice."

"We should go back," Harper says. "He's—"

"No." I squeeze her hand tighter. My gut tells me running back to him would be the biggest mistake we could make. "I think he's trying to make us feel bad."

"But he just promised to bring us home."

"And you believe that? He's still threatening to hurt us. What makes you think he won't hurt us anyway if we go back?"

Through the darkness, I see her face crumple. "I just want to go home. I'm so over this."

My chest tightens. "I know. Me too. That's why we have to keep going."

The beam of a flashlight shines through the gaps in the trees, signaling that he's getting closer. If we move now, he'll hear us. I hold my breath and tug Harper and Levi closer. "These woods are dangerous," says Dad. "You'll get lost if you keep going, especially in the dark. It doesn't have to be this way."

My gaze follows the flashlight as it continues to the left of us. He's going in the opposite direction, but it's too early to feel relieved. I need to make sure he doesn't turn around before I make my next move. While I wait, I'll have to decide what my next move is in the first place; I don't know these woods. I don't know where they lead, and I certainly don't know how long it'll take to get us out of here. What I *do* know is that somehow, we need to follow the road while maintaining enough distance that Dad won't see us if he takes the BMW.

We'll have to go right of the cottage, back the way we came to get here. I don't know if there are any other cottages further down the road, and it's a risk we can't afford to take. My mind is made up; we're going to our old cottage—or one of the other two next to it—and knocking on their door.

The only downside is that it's going to be a *long* walk.

"All I wanted was to keep you safe, and you're not safe out here. You can come back; I won't be mad. I promise you'll get to see Mom next week." His voice is faint, now; perfect.

A gentle breeze makes its way to us, rustling the leaves above. It's go time. "Come on," I whisper, and rise to my feet. "Don't run just yet. Tiptoe until I say so."

"Where are we going?" Levi asks.

"Back to our old cottage. It's far, I know, but we have to."

The light disappears as we begin to walk. When my eyes have fully adjusted to the pitch-black, I can just barely make out the road to the far right of us, quiet as ever. As we step over fallen trees and leaves, I brief Harper and Levi on my new plan. "But what if no one answers the door at the cottages?" Harper asks.

I shrug. "There's three of them. And there was a car in the driveway of our old cottage when we went by a few days ago, so if we're loud enough, one of them should. It's also summer break now, so maybe the others have shown up for camp. But if not, we keep going until we get to the next set of cottages."

Another gunshot rings through the air, cutting through the silence, and I jump. *He's wasting bullets*, I can't help but think. He starts to speak, but he's hard to hear now. *Wasting his breath, too.*

Let him. Hopefully it won't be long before he realizes he's wasting his time, too.

CHAPTER 17

"We should be running," Harper declares. "Why aren't we running?"

"We don't need to," I say. "We have enough distance."

What I don't tell her is that I'm absolutely terrified. Older sisters are supposed to be brave, but I feel the complete opposite. I've been on the brink of a mental breakdown for the last few hours, faking confidence in the scariest moments of my life. The only thing motivating me to keep going is the realization that if I stop, we might die. Then all of this will have been for nothing.

I suspect we've lost him by now, but he might have some tricks up his sleeve we don't know about. The thought makes my pulse spike. I can't stand how unpredictable this night is.

A tickle spreads across my face, and my body comes alive with fear at the realization that I've just walked through a spiderweb. I bite back a scream and instinctively swat at my upper body. Isn't it interesting how we've been reduced to prey in the woods, being hunted by Dad and his gun, and I'm concerned about a freaking *spider* being on me?

"What happened?" says Harper, a hint of alarm in her voice.

"Just a spiderweb." I spit on the ground. "Nothing to worry about."

Tears gather in my eyes, and I angrily wipe them away. If I'd been quieter in the cottage, maybe I would have found the BMW keys and prevented this stupid night hike through the forest. We could be at the police station by now, with Mom on her way to pick us up. It's so goddamn unfair. I've worked so hard the last couple days to make this escape plan easy, and now I have to make it up as I go. I don't have a contingency plan if things go wrong. We might be screwed.

Crickets chirp around us, and branches snap in every direction. For all I know, a bear could be two feet from us, waiting for its moment to strike. I shudder as a memory from three years ago resurfaces; hiking in Yellowstone National Park with my family as a bear followed close behind us on the trail, seemingly stalking us. I still remember how my spine tingled with the familiar feeling of being watched, and how painfully aware I was that there was absolutely nothing I could do about it. Aunt Annie begged us to stay calm. "Whatever you do, *don't run*. Right now, he's more scared of you than you are of him." Whether that was true, I didn't know. He wandered back into the woods five minutes later, but it felt like hours.

I've never been a fan of hiking, especially not since that day. And I'd never have the guts to run through the forest like this in the daytime, let alone in the middle of the night.

"Alyssa, I'm scared," Levi whines for the millionth time tonight.

I feel like a parent; how do they manage to push aside their own fears for the sake of comforting their kids time and time again? "It's going to be okay, Levi."

"How much longer?"

"I don't know."

"I can't see. It's *so* dark out. I wish we had a flashlight."

"That makes two of us, Levi. But Dad has my phone."

Oh, how easy things would be if I had my phone. All I'd have to do is call 911 and wait close enough to the road to see them coming. It's yet another luxury I've taken for granted.

A pair of bright, white headlights appear on the road, and the car slows to a stop parallel to us, as if knowing exactly where we are. Dad steps out of the car, and within seconds, I hear the click of the gun. He doesn't fire yet. "The forecast is calling for thunderstorms," he says. "You don't want to be stuck outside. At least come warm up inside the car. Like I said, I'll take you home next week. Final offer. I know you don't believe me."

I crouch as low as I can to the ground as he swivels his head left, right, left, right, blindly searching for us. "I know you're scared," he continues. "You've never liked the dark. But you don't need to be scared, because I'll be right here, following you. I know exactly where you're going, and besides, I have help on the way."

My blood turns cold. *No.*

I'm backed into a corner, with no way out. Those three cottages were our only hope. How could I have been stupid enough to think he wouldn't know we were heading there?

I need a new plan, but we might be officially out of options. Looks like we'll have to surrender anyway.

No. Absolutely not. I mentally kick myself for even considering that an option. We can't give up after all the work that's gone into this escape plan. We'll have to come up with something else, but this time, we don't have time on our side.

"Just thought I'd let you know," Dad says with a hint of a smile in his voice. "See you there."

The sound of the car door slamming rings in my ears, and my eyes fill to the brim. I sink further into the earth and bury my head in my hands, then dig my fingers through my scalp until the pain starts. The weight of defeat spreads through my body like a cancer. "I don't know what to do next," I admit.

Harper kneels next to me. "What if we split up? When Dad is gone, we can go back to his cottage and look for our phones."

I laugh hollowly. "We can't split up. Every horror movie ever made has proved that's a bad idea."

"We could all go back to the cottage, then?"

"I don't think that's a good idea, either. Dad never specified how much help he has. For all we know, someone's in there right now."

"But no other cars have gone by."

She makes a good point, but it's still too risky. "I know, but someone else could be showing up any minute and catch us there." I get back to my feet and wipe the dirt from my bare legs. "Come on, let's keep going. We're not accomplishing anything by sitting around like ducks."

More branches snap at once; there's an animal close by. We need to get out of here. And we're going to run this time.

With no clear path cut out for us, running is more difficult than I expected. It's like practicing the hurdles in gym class, only the ground is uneven and bare branches slice at my skin. Despite lacking a clear plan, I lead the way toward the three cottages anyway; I'll have plenty of time to brainstorm our next moves along the journey. For now, my only goal is pushing forward. I don't have anyone to tell me what the right thing to do is, so I can only hope that I'm not about to make things even worse.

A cramp forms in my side, and I struggle to take air into my lungs. Books make this seem so easy; how do characters seem to have all the energy in the world when they're running away? Adrenaline? Pure luck? Superior athleticism? I'll bet even the authors don't know. Fiction doesn't have to be realistic, I guess.

Man, I should have practiced running more back at home. Maybe Mom was on to something with those workouts she tried forcing on me. She might be proud of me.

No, that's incredibly toxic. She shouldn't have been so worried about me gaining weight when it's a perfectly normal part of growing up.

But exercise is also good for your health.

God, shut up, brain. No one cares.

My foot collides with a tree root, and before I can process what's happened, I'm flat on my stomach on the forest floor. Dirt cakes under my fingernails. White hot pain explodes up my ankle, and stars dance across my vision. *Great. Just great.*

"Oh my God, are you okay?" Harper's hand is suddenly on my shoulder. "Can you get up?"

I pick myself up off the ground, and when I transfer some weight to my ankle, I almost scream. I lean against a tree and suck air in through my teeth. "I think I sprained my ankle. This is *not* good."

"What are we gonna do, then?" Levi asks.

"How am I supposed to know?" Without warning, I burst into tears. Fat, ugly sobs that rack my whole body. It catches me off guard, but now that I've started, I can't stop. We're doomed.

I can't run away now. How am I supposed to do that when I can't even walk?

"Sit down for a few minutes," says Harper, directing me to a fallen tree. I lower myself onto the trunk and swipe at my wet eyes. "It probably just needs rest. Remember when I thought I broke my ankle last year in the yard and it turns out I was just being a baby?"

A smile forces its way into my misery. "Wow, thanks Harper."

"I'm not saying *you're* being a baby. I'm saying you need to give it time."

"But we don't really have time."

The sky lights up, then, and a crackle of thunder sounds in the distance; the perfect weather to match my mood. Great. I throw my hood over my head to shield myself from the rain that'll soon be dumping over us. We'll wait out the worst of the storm here before proceeding. The car has crept further up the road, anticipating that we've continued walking, and somehow that comforts me a little. He really has no idea where we are. We could use that to our advantage.

Only, I don't really know how.

I sniffle and take a few deep breaths. *You're going to be fine. It's just a bump in the road.* If I tell this to myself enough times, maybe it'll make it true.

Thanks for Meeting Today!

Melissa Bennett <bennettfamofficial@gmail.com>
Hi Pete,
Just wanted to come on here and say thank you for meeting with me this afternoon. It really means a lot to me that you took the time out of your busy day to provide that information. I think it's going to be so helpful in this case.
Thanks once again, and if you remember anything else, please don't hesitate to reach out.
Sincerely,
Melissa

Pete Bucknell <peter.bucknell.89@gmail.com>
Hi Melissa,
I'm happy I could help. Hopefully this brings us one step closer to locating your children. This whole situation has shaken me to my core and made me realize that I truly don't know some people the way I thought I did. I can't imagine how you're feeling.
It was nice seeing you after such a long time. Once your children are home and you have settled back into routine, it would be awesome if we could catch up for a coffee sometime.
Pete

Melissa Bennett <bennettfamofficial@gmail.com>
Absolutely, that would be wonderful! It's been a while since we've caught up. How have you been, otherwise? I didn't really get the chance to ask you earlier.

Pete Bucknell <peter.bucknell.89@gmail.com>

I've been all right. We can talk about me more when we meet up, but right now, your kids are a top priority. I'll be here whenever you feel ready! Take all the time you need, and if you need help with anything, you know I'll be there.

Melissa Bennett <bennettfamofficial@gmail.com>
Thank you so much, Pete! I appreciate it more than you know. I'll see you then, whenever that is. And please don't tell anyone about our past and that we know each other. I don't want people finding out.

Pete Bucknell <peter.bucknell.89@gmail.com>
You've got it. My lips are sealed.

CHAPTER 18
LAST YEAR

After spending the last few weeks driving around the United States, we're finally homebound.

For this annual March Break trip, Mom initially wanted to visit New York City again, since it's been almost ten years since we've gone, but Dad desperately wanted to travel the famous Route 66 Highway, so here we are. It took over forty hours of driving to get to Los Angeles, and now that we've been exploring the city for a while, it's time to drive *another* forty hours to get back home. I can't say I'm too excited about the drive, but it's pretty scenic, so I can't complain. I also get to miss school, which is another bonus.

As the hustle and bustle of the big city gives way to rolling hills, I lean back in my seat, slipping my headphones over my ears. Reading in the car makes me nauseous, so I've opted for an audiobook; a YA romance about a quarterback falling for the quiet, studious girl with no friends. Cliché, I know, but a guilty pleasure nonetheless. When you're the one with no friends (aside from Cara), it's nice to fantasize about the possibility of boys actually paying you any attention.

Before I can get into the audiobook, my phone pings with an Instagram notification. I've been tagged in Mom's newest post; a photo of the five of us standing in front of the Hollywood sign, grinning wide. It's captioned, *Hollywood, baby!* Likes and comments start pouring in immediately, but before I can get too engrossed in them, I switch apps and start the book. It has become a bit of an unhealthy obsession of mine lately, reading every single comment that comes in, good or bad. The fans have started to suspect my parents are having issues in their marriage, and the comments haven't been all that positive. If we get enough of them, we're going to have to address it, and that could go one of two ways: drama channels will start posting divorce rumors, or there will be a scandal.

I despise both options.

"So, we've officially hit the road," I hear Mom say to the vlog camera. "I can't believe our vacation is already coming to an end. I always dread this part, but at the end of the day, we have *so* many amazing memories to look back on." She pans the camera to the three of us in the back seat. "Anyone have a favourite part of the trip they'd like to share?"

"Disneyland!" Levi pipes up. "And the Walk of Fame and the beach and the—"

"The whole road trip was awesome, but I loved seeing the desert," says Harper. "We should do another trip after this."

"We don't have the money for that," Dad grumbles.

I pause the audiobook as Mom directs her attention—and her camera—toward me. "What about you, Lissy? Any trip highlights you want to mention?"

I groan inwardly and lift the headphones off, placing them in my lap. "Um, I liked the Santa Monica Pier. That was fun."

"Anything else?"

I shrug. "I mean, I had fun overall. I liked seeing so many new places in one trip."

She beams. "Me too. And you, Dan?" She pivots the camera toward Dad. "What was your favourite part of the trip?"

"Get that camera off me," he says sharply. "I don't want to be filmed right now."

She sighs heavily and shuts the camera off. "Wow. Thanks for ruining the footage."

"Oh, stop being so dramatic. You can cut that part out if it bothers you so much."

"People are going to think you're—"

"You think I give a shit what other people think?" His loud voice cuts like a knife, and he slaps the steering wheel. "Seriously? Why would I waste my time worrying about whether total strangers like me? Why should I give your little 'fans' the time of day?"

Oh Lord, here we go. I'd put the headphones back on and ignore them, but if history repeats itself, they're going to yell so much that it'll be impossible to tune out. I lean forward and sink my head into my hands.

"They're *our* fans, Dan, and we have an image to keep up," Mom snaps back. "These videos pay the bills. In case you haven't noticed, my 'little' videos have made us millions and allowed us to take trips like this in the first place!"

"Do you even hear yourself? *'We have an image to keep up.'* Do you know how disgusting that sounds? We're just going to spend the rest of our lives living for other people?"

Tears track down Mom's cheeks. "That's not what it means."

"That's exactly what it means. And I'm sorry, but I don't want you dragging our kids into this mess anymore. I don't want them to grow up thinking they have to constantly be perfect for other people's approval."

"I'm not dragging them into anything!" She whips around to face us. "You guys like being in videos, don't you? You have fun doing them?"

Harper, Levi and I exchange glances, but Dad doesn't give us time to respond. "Don't tell them what they like, Melissa! You force them to take part in these videos. They don't know any different, and I don't want them on the internet anymore."

My ears perk up. If Dad can successfully talk some sense into her, I'll never have to show my face on the channel again, and the thought brings a jolt of excitement through me. I don't want to get my hopes up, but a girl can dream. I know after the period video that Harper will be ecstatic, too. I sit up and lean against the glass, pretending to watch the hills and trees pass by.

"I'm not stopping something I enjoy," Mom weeps.

"You might enjoy it, but no one else does." Dad shakes his head and lowers his voice slightly. "The kids have been on the internet their whole lives. Levi and Harper have had Instagram accounts since before they were born. I didn't understand much about social media before, but the more I'm learning about it, the more it doesn't feel safe anymore. Especially after that stalker we had."

What? I can't stop the gasp that leaves my throat. "Stalker?" I blurt.

"You mean some guy was creeping on us and you didn't tell us?" says Harper.

"It was a woman." Dad sighs heavily. "It was a few months ago, and it's been dealt with, but yes, we had a stalker. She—"

"We weren't supposed to tell them." Mom throws up her hands. "Now you're just going to make them paranoid."

Dad continues as if he didn't hear her. "She claimed to be our 'biggest fan' and found out where we lived. She saw the 'for sale' sign in the background of a video, when the neighbours sold their house. She drove all the way—"

"Enough, Dan," Mom warns.

"—from Pennsylvania to get here, followed me to work, followed your bus to school. Called my office pretending to be a relative and told him there was a family emergency, just so I would leave work and she would run into me. We had the police involved, and luckily it ended there, but I don't know what her intentions were. She could have planned to kidnap you three for all I know."

Nausea overtakes me as I digest what he's just told me. Someone followed me on my bus one day, and I had no idea. We didn't know she existed, but she knew everything about us, things we didn't even share on the internet. Maybe she wanted to hurt or kill us. I shiver in disgust. I've never felt so vulnerable in my life.

And it's Mom's fault.

I don't even know what to say.

Dad fills the silence for us. "This isn't the first time we've had people obsess over us and try to interfere with our lives, but it was the first time someone got that close to us. And I don't want to experience that ever again. Which is why this needs to end now."

"We need to stop focusing so much on the negatives." Mom wipes her eyes. "Play the what-if game all you want, but the way I see it, she never harmed us, nor has anyone."

"You don't count the kids being bullied in school as being harmed?"

"I don't want to talk about this anymore. I already told you the other day, those bullies should learn to be nicer. I'll talk to their parents when we get home if it helps."

Panic consumes me. "No! Please don't talk to Laurel and Jessica's parents. Please. That won't help."

It would make it a million times worse, guaranteed. They'd have something new to make fun of; me being a baby running to my mommy, crying about how mean everyone is. I don't know what the solution is, but it can't be that.

"Well, they need to know that their kids are being jerks," Mom argues.

"Mom, no. I can deal with it myself. Just don't say anything."

"And don't tell Caleb's parents, either," Harper chimes in.

Mom shakes her head, and doesn't say anything; just picks up her camera and starts to film some b-roll footage of the scenery.

***

After a long day of driving and fighting, we finally stop for the night in Santa Fe just after midnight. The cool night air greets me as I step out of the car, and *man*, it feels good to stretch my legs. The weight of exhaustion presses against my eyelids, reminding me that it's way past my usual bedtime.

Levi doesn't wake up, so Mom carries him into the hotel, and I follow behind sluggishly. While Dad checks us in, Mom manages to sneak a few more clips in from her iPhone; a view of the glowing hotel sign, Levi dozing against her shoulder, Dad speaking with the staff, Harper yawning. Dad won't be happy when he sees the footage on YouTube later, but then again, I don't think he watches our videos much anymore. I don't, either.

When we get to our room, I dive straight into bed, too tired to change into my pajamas or brush my teeth. It's been a long day, and we have at least two more of these ahead of us before we're finally home. Harper joins me, falling asleep almost instantly, and Mom tucks Levi into the cot next to our bed. Neither of my parents make an effort to come to bed just yet, even after they've turned out all the lights and the room has plunged into darkness. Mom pulls up a chair in the corner and opens her laptop, preparing for a quick edit before bed.

That's when the whispering starts.

"It's almost one in the morning," Dad says. "Put that away."

"I'm not bothering anyone, am I?"

"You have all day tomorrow to edit in the car. I don't want you waking up the kids."

Mom huffs and slams the laptop closed. "You're being ridiculous, Dan. Why have you been attacking me all day? Do you really hate me this much?"

I steal a glance at my parents in the far corner of the dark room, and Dad rests a hand on Mom's shoulder. "I don't hate *you*, Mel. We've been over this a million times. I hate what you do."

Looks like I won't be sleeping anytime soon. It's far from the first time this conversation has happened, and it's only going to escalate from here. I huff in frustration and roll over a little too aggressively, hoping they'll get the hint that I can hear them, but it doesn't work.

"I just want your support." Her voice is thick with tears. "You seem to hate everything I love."

"I don't. But I can't support something that puts us in danger. Especially involving our kids."

"Nothing bad is going to happen."

"You don't know that."

Mom sniffs. "I think I want a divorce."

My heart slams in my ribcage. *Oh my God.* This is it, the end they've been hinting at for the last few months. Mom dissolves into sobs, and I hold my breath as I wait for Dad's response. Nothing good can come out of this.

To my surprise, he laughs. And not just a short chuckle; a loud belly laugh that has him doubling over, fighting for air. Harper stirs at the sound. "Do you now?" he wheezes. "My God, what will the viewers think?"

"Dan—"

"Think of the views we'll get on our 'announcing our divorce' video! We'll break the internet!"

"It's not funny," Mom snaps. "Nice to see this is all some big joke to you."

"Because it is. You *think* you want a divorce, or do you actually want a divorce?"

"I want one."

"So, how do we spice up the video? Do we cry big, fake tears for sympathy points? Make shocked faces for the thumbnail?"

"*Dan!* Cut it out! You're going to wake the kids."

"A bit late for that. I know they're pretending to sleep."

I squeeze my eyes shut tighter. I'm facing away from Mom now, but I sense her staring.

"Great," she says. "What a terrible way for them to find out."

"Whatever. I'm going to bed. We have to be up early."

It's then that I realize our family will never be the same again.

CHAPTER 19
NOW

When the rain comes, it's merciless.

What begins as a few fat droplets quickly becomes a torrential downpour, and the trees sway in the gusts of wind. Roaring thunder drowns out the sounds of the forest around us. I hug my knees to my chest and shiver, silently thanking Harper for her brilliant idea of making us wear sweaters. Sometimes I wonder what I'd do without her.

The harder it rains, the tighter the knot in my stomach gets. I've never been a fan of thunderstorms, and never in a million years did I think I'd sit outside in one. I'd make a beeline for our basement while everyone else would remain glued to the picture windows in our living room, watching with fascination as the sky blackened. For all I know, we could have a tornado warning right now; Southern Ontario summer weather does get pretty unpredictable. The basement is the safest place to be in a storm like this, away from windows and outside walls. Despite that, I obviously can't accept Dad's offer.

My ankle throbs, reminding me that my options are limited. I'll let it rest as we ride out the storm, but when the rain stops, I'll need to press forward, no matter how blinding the pain is. I can't sit out here and wait for someone to rescue us. That responsibility has fallen into my own hands.

A small tree crashes down feet from us and we jump. Levi screams and clutches me tighter, burying his face in my shoulder. "We're okay," I tell him, ruffling his hair.

"I forgot to bring Snuggles," he whimpers.

Snuggles. That freaking teddy bear he's so attached to. "It's okay. Someone will get him for you when we're home."

"Can we go back? *Pleeease?*"

"We can't, buddy. You know that. He's safe where he is."

He releases a heart-wrenching sob. "But I need him."

We absolutely cannot go back just for a teddy bear. "It's only for a few hours. You'll get him back, I promise."

We've covered enough ground now that I can't see the cottage anymore, and to be honest, I'm not sure I know the way back. We're fully committed, now. "Besides, at least we know where he is," I add. "You wouldn't want to lose Snuggles out here in the woods. We'd never find him again."

Levi sniffles. "Okay."

"So we'll keep going once the storm is over. We'll be home before you know it."

An idea forms in my head. We shouldn't be too far from the lake, and from what I remember, it's not a very wide lake. If we follow the shoreline instead of the road, we might have a better chance of being hidden. Instead of going to our old cottage, we might be able to find a canoe and cross the water, or wait until morning and flag down a boater. I'm not sure what time it is, but the sun will probably be up in a few hours, so we won't need to wait long. It's worth a shot.

I don't recall seeing the lake from Pete's cottage, but I know it's nearby. And if Pete had a boat, we may have missed our opportunity to steal it.

Don't think like that. The shoreline is mostly a straight stretch, and when we get there, I might be able to see Pete's dock in the distance. If there's a boat there, we're going for it.

Since Dad is in the BMW, there's no way he could have snagged this theoretical boat, but the jury is still out as to whether or not there's someone else who could have. Someone helping Dad find us. There's only one way to find out, and it's not from sitting here obsessing over the what-ifs.

The rain hasn't quite calmed yet, but I push myself to my feet and transfer some weight onto my bad foot, wincing at the sharp pain. It feels like thumbtacks puncturing through my skin, but admittedly, it's improved. I should be fine to walk, but I'll have to pace myself; I want to be able to run if need be. I bend and touch my ankle, and sure enough, there's a sizable bump there. I'm confident it's not broken now that I'm standing, but I'll likely be spending a good chunk of my summer hobbling around on crutches.

Bummer.

"We're leaving already?" Harper shouts over the rain. "I thought we were waiting here until the storm was done?"

Lightning streaks across the sky, providing me with enough light to catch a brief glimpse of her face. I convince myself her red eyes are from the rain. "We'll wait. I just want to put some weight on this ankle first."

"How is it, now?"

I shrug. "Could be better. Could be worse."

Rain drips from my hood into my eyes, and I swipe at it, smearing the cold water across my face. The trees don't provide much shelter, so I'm completely drenched, my clothes stuck to my body. As the temperature continues to drop, the more unbearable the feeling becomes. Dreams of soft blankets and a hot shower dance in my head, taunting me, reminding me of what I don't have, and it strikes a nerve somewhere inside me. I shouldn't have to do this. I shouldn't have to traipse through the woods in search of safety from my own flesh and blood. I shouldn't have to risk my life outside in a severe thunderstorm when I should be tucked away safely in bed. I shouldn't have to wonder whether or not I'm going to die trying to save us. I shouldn't have to take part in this sick mental game where I have to decide which parent is better, when both of them have done some fucked-up things.

I shouldn't be here. But like I have done my whole life, I'm forced to do yet another thing I don't want to do.

I may have chosen to run away, but I didn't ask to be kidnapped. I didn't ask to have my life exploited in front of millions. And I didn't ask to have to try to fix it.

I gesture to my siblings. "Let's go."

***

As the rain slows to a drizzle, we trek along blindly through the dark of night. Puddles cover the forest floor, but I don't notice them until my feet sink into one, filling my shoes, the water rising past my ankles. When I yank my feet free, mud cakes my soles, and water squishes between my toes with each step. I grit my teeth. "This sucks," I grumble.

Unfortunately, it's already too late for Harper and Levi to avoid the same puddle, and Harper nearly loses her balance. "Ugh, what the fuck!"

"Harper, we've been through this. Don't—"

"Don't what, swear? Well, guess what? I'm soaked to the fucking bone. Does that not matter? And why do you get to swear and I don't?"

I snort. This kid is something else. "I'm older."

"So? You're still not an adult."

"Whatever. We can talk about this another time, when we're not lost."

I try to pass it off as a joke, but panic threatens to engulf me the more we walk. We've been walking for half an hour, and somehow we still haven't reached the water. I can't tell which direction we're travelling anymore. My eyes have somewhat adjusted to the darkness, but even still, we should be seeing the lake even from a distance. Is it possible we're going the wrong way?

We're lost. *We're lost we're lost we're lost.*

Nothing is going as planned. I should've known that would happen.

"Are we lost?" Levi asks.

"Nope," I say too quickly. "We're almost there."

"You said that a long time ago."

"Well this time, we are."

Branches crunch to our left, and when I turn my head in response to the noise, I recoil so hard I almost topple over yet again. The silhouette of a bear makes its way toward the puddle we stood at moments ago, just behind us. I hold my breath, remembering the Yellowstone trip, how my skin prickled with fear. Harper and Levi notice the bear, too, and just as Levi prepares to scream, I yank him closer and shove my hand over his mouth. "Shh. Don't."

"What do we do?" Harper whimpers.

I try to remember what Aunt Annie told us on that trip three years ago. "Don't run," I repeat. "He's more scared of us than we are of him."

Do we stay still and risk him seeing us? Or do we keep going and risk him hearing us? Are all bears scared of humans, or will this one be different? My brain becomes so overwhelmed with the possibilities that I feel trapped in my own skin, unable to move, unable to think. I want to curl into a ball and do nothing, but as my heart pounds an unsteady rhythm in my chest, I'm reminded that I don't have that option. I have to make a decision before it's too late.

"Keep walking, but go slow," I tell my siblings, my voice barely a whisper. I guide them along, making sure I don't turn my back, and hope they don't notice the way my breath quickens. I can only hope this decision is the right one.

Time and time again over the last couple days, I've found myself in disbelief that all of this is real. Things like this happen to other people, people on true crime shows and survival shows; not people like me. I can't take the easy way out right now and simply close my eyes, waking up in bed drenched in sweat, the bear only a figment of my imagination. My life has become a living nightmare, and I need to learn to survive.

A twig snaps under my foot, breaking through the deafening silence like a thunderclap. The bear's head swivels in our direction, and time freezes. *He sees us.* Goosebumps dance across my flesh, and instinctively I duck, pulling Harper and Levi down with me. I press a finger to my lips, a sharp warning.

The bear's gaze meets mine, and before I have the chance to react, it takes off running in the opposite direction.

I'm so relieved I could cry.

"That was the most terrifying few minutes of my life," Harper says as we get back up and continue on our way. "That thing could have eaten us all for breakfast, and all of this would have been for nothing."

An unexpected laugh bubbles in my chest. "Guess we didn't look appetizing enough."

"What if there are others, though? What if his little bear friends are out looking for a snack right now?"

"Hopefully they skip us."

"This is the part where you're supposed to tell me there *are* no bear friends looking for us."

"I was joking, Harper." I pull one of my wet shoes and socks off, wringing the sock out over the grass. My hand grazes the bump on my ankle, sending another shockwave of pain through me. "Ugh, this is so gross."

A chilly breeze floats over us, and my teeth chatter. I have nowhere to wipe the mud on my hands, so I brush them across my bare thighs, feeling the raised skin where the branches scraped me. I have no doubt I'm probably bleeding somewhere. Add that to the laundry list of things that would normally concern me, but I don't have the capacity to worry about tonight.

"Alyssa, look!" Harper cries. She's pointing to something up ahead. "The water!"

I look up from the ground and, sure enough, we've made it. The lake sits ahead of us in all its glory, waiting for us. *Thank God.* We're not lost after all.

Now it's time to find that boat.

CHAPTER 20

"The mosquitos are *soooo* bad," Levi whines. He dramatically swipes at the air. "They're biting me everywhere!"

They are, indeed, biting us everywhere. My legs itch like crazy; bug spray would be a lifesaver right now. I do wish, though, that Levi would stop complaining. "It did just rain, Levi. They'll probably go away."

"I want them to go away right now!" He slaps his leg, killing one. "I hate this!"

"That makes two of us," I mutter. I hoist myself over a fallen tree, and at last, make it to the shoreline.

The clouds begin to part overhead, and a sliver of moonlight peeks through. Gentle waves lap at my feet, the sound calming amidst the chaos of tonight. I glance straight ahead at the water, at the cottages on the other side that are bathed in darkness. It's not a wide lake, but the cottages are definitely too far to swim to. Of course, there's nothing surrounding me I could use as a makeshift boat, so we're down to one option: find a real boat.

When Dad used to have a motorboat, he always kept the paddles tucked inside it somewhere. I'm hoping, if we find a boat, its owners will have done the same. And forgive us for stealing it.

I'm sure they would if they knew what we were going through.

First I look left, back where we came from. I can see the outline of Pete's dock protruding onto the lake, but disappointment weighs heavy in my stomach as I see there's no boat. "Ugh," I mutter. "Of course there isn't."

"There isn't what?" Harper asks.

"A boat on Pete's dock. I wanted to take it across the water to get help."

She sighs. "Yeah, that *does* suck. But at least we've made it pretty far."

She's right; we've covered a great amount of distance. If I had to guess, maybe a kilometer or two. I look to my right, now, to see how far we have left to go, and am just as disappointed. "We're still really far from the other cottages, though."

"I thought we were trying to come up with a different plan and avoid the cottages altogether?"

"This *was* the plan, Harper. Now we need another one."

Something has to go right tonight; I don't know how many more dead ends I can handle. A mosquito buzzes incessantly in my ear, and I swing at it, cursing under my breath. *Deep breaths, Alyssa. Calm the heck down.*

"There might be a canoe or kayak at the cottage," says Harper. "If Pete had a deck, they might be under it or something."

I mentally kick myself for not being quieter in the kitchen; we might have otherwise had time to check for those things before we left. "He might, but it's a waste of time to go all the way back there now. It would've been worth it if he had a boat. But if we go there and it turns out he only has one kayak, all three of us won't fit in it, and we're not leaving anyone behind."

"True. So now what? We keep walking?"

"We have to."

So, we do. It's much easier to stick to the shoreline as we walk; the ground is mostly even, and the fallen branches are tucked away. We're well hidden from the road. For now, it's also keeping us from getting lost since we can clearly see where we're going now. The only problem is that Dad knows it's where we planned to go; he just doesn't know when we'll get there.

He'll wait as long as it takes if it means he gets to keep us locked in his basement, away from Mom.

We could try approaching our old cottage from the back door, but will Dad see us cross the yards? Or worse, does he somehow have access to the cottage and will be waiting for us inside?

At this rate, my brain will explode if I keep thinking.

"Do you think this will be worth it?" Harper asks, breaking our silence. "Like, if we can make it home, do you think Mom will stop the channel?"

While my focus has mostly been on sending Dad to jail, it's another question I haven't been able to stop thinking about. I hope to God, with all my might, that tonight's escape will fix things on both sides. "I really hope so," I answer, brushing another mosquito off my thigh.

My skin begins to tingle. "Or, at the very least, I hope she slows down on vlogging. I'm sure she'll take into account that it's become a huge problem."

It occurs to me, now, that this is the longest I have gone without being filmed in *years*. Probably my whole life. Everything has been documented, from my first tooth to my first steps to each meal I've eaten in a day. It's a strange feeling, not having to talk to a camera during what I'd consider to be a huge event in my life right now, because I've never gone without doing it. I imagine vlogging this very moment, and if it weren't for the exhaustion, I'd crack up: *What's up Bennett FamJams, it's Alyssa, and today's vlog is a little different. Come with me while I run away from my dad!*

"But our fans are gonna miss us," says Levi. "Mom said lots of them have been watching us for seventeen years."

"Yep, they have." A weird and unfortunate reality. If I had a dollar for every time a stranger approached me in public and told me they couldn't believe how grown up I was, that they'd watched me since I'd been in diapers, I'd never have to work a day in my life. "But we can't keep living our lives for them. It's ruined ours. It's the reason behind this entire kidnapping thing. And now we're forever going to be known as Those Vlogger Kids That Were Kidnapped by Their Dad."

Harper groans. "Great. That'll give people more reason to bully us at school."

"Exactly. So if this doesn't make her stop, I don't know what will."

This was Dad's goal by taking us—to make her stop the channel—but he ultimately chose the worst way to do it. He wasn't giving us any freedom. I'm going to show him that I don't need his help ending this once and for all, and that choosing revenge over our safety was the biggest mistake he could make.

"I wonder how she's going to make money if she quits." Harper kicks a rock out of her way.

"I'm sure she has savings. After that runs out, I don't know. There are probably tons of other jobs where she can work from home."

"Do you think she'll let us visit Dad in jail?"

I snort. Leave it to Harper to worry about something like that. "I don't know. But one thing's for sure; I'm not visiting."

"Me neither."

"Me three," Levi pipes up.

Considering the distance we still have left to travel, I have plenty of time to think of another plan for getting out of here. So far, the only place I can think to go is the cottage, and if we still decide to do that, I'm hoping it'll still be dark out so it'll be easier to hide. Maybe if Dad parks outside the cottage for too long, the owners will be suspicious and call the police. Besides, his license plate is probably plastered all over the news, and if we can stall long enough, someone might drive by and recognize it. Maybe it's better to wait it out, after all.

Regardless of what we decide to do, we can't camp out where we are right now. I want us to be found sooner rather than later by the police.

I know Dad didn't plan for us to run away, so he's making things up as he goes along, just like we are. And I plan to use that to my advantage.

NEW VIDEO FROM THEBENNETTFAM
CHAT WITH SOFIA LOPEZ - HELP BRING MY KIDS HOME!

Good morning Bennett FamJams, and welcome back to the channel. I truly believe that we are so, so, SO close to finding Alyssa, Harper and Levi, and it's all because of the hard work of our local police department and you guys, who have been sending tips in like crazy. I can't say it enough times, but THANK YOU!

Before I bring on today's guest, I just want to recap everything we know so far after chatting with Pete Bucknell. The police have also told me they're looking into traffic light cameras surrounding our town, and so far, they've been able to track some of Dan's movements as far as two hours away from here. I can't share much on that end, but why don't we go ahead and talk about some of the things Pete mentioned?

If you didn't watch the last video, I chatted with Pete Bucknell, who was an old coworker of Dan's. The morning the kids were taken, Dan suddenly quit his job without giving any sort of notice. Very sudden and unlike him. But Pete also says Dan raved constantly about wanting to move to Mexico just before taking the kids, which leads us to believe that he may have somehow illegally crossed the border with the kids. After I published that video, Sofia Lopez, who currently lives in Mexico, reached out to me via email with some information she believes is important. So I've just connected with her via Zoom so she can talk about it with us today. Sofia, why don't you go ahead and introduce yourself?

Sofia: Hi Melissa! Thank you so much for having me on the channel today. I'm a huge fan and have literally been watching your videos since you started the channel! I've watched every single video you've ever posted, and I can't believe I get to finally meet you. Also, hi to everyone watching as well! My name is Sofia, and I live near Puerto Vallarta in Mexico. After watching the last video, it made me *remember something I saw a few days ago that I didn't think much of, but with Pete's insight, now it has me thinking I wasn't crazy.*

Melissa: *Can you please explain what it was you saw?*

Sofia: *I was walking along the beach the other day, and saw a guy playing with his kids in the ocean. I could have sworn it was Dan and the kids, but lots of people probably look like Dan, or Alyssa or Harper or Levi. There was no way my favourite YouTubers were here, close to where I live, especially when they were considered actively missing. But then Pete said Dan wanted to move to Mexico. I think maybe he took them to Puerto Vallarta, and I really did see them. Plus, Canadians take vacations here all the time.*

Melissa: *Yes, we've been to Puerto Vallarta before, actually. Can you describe what they were doing? Or even what they were wearing, if you can remember?*

Sofia: *Um, well, like I said, they were just playing in the ocean, tossing a beach ball around. The teenage girl I could have sworn was Alyssa. She had a glittery blue swimsuit on, which I'm pretty sure I saw her wearing in her last try-on haul.*

Melissa: *Could you hear them from where you were standing? Did they talk about anything, or were they just playing?*

Sofia: *I couldn't hear much, to be honest, but they were definitely talking. I heard snippets about the weather. I think they said something about Canada once or twice.*

Melissa: *What was their demeanor like? Did they seem happy? Sad or angry at any point?*

Sofia: *Mostly happy. But the dad got mad at the younger girl over pushing her brother in the water. I don't know if that helps.*

Melissa: *Um, well any piece of information, no matter how small it might seem, could be important, so it's good to know. How long ago was this?*

Sofia: *Hmm, let me think. It was, like, yesterday afternoon.*

Melissa: *And, sorry, I can't remember if I asked you this already, but what did they look like? Did they look to be in the same age ranges as the kids? Hair colours? Same build?*

Sofia: *Yeah, like I said, I totally thought it was them. Teenage girl with long, brown hair. Pre-teen girl with brown hair. Little boy with blond hair. The dad was wearing a hat, so I couldn't really tell, especially from a distance, but I think he had dark hair, too. Their voices sounded kinda similar to what I've heard on your channel before. At least, what I was able to hear of their conversation.*

Melissa: Okay. It's definitely something I will mention to the police because, like I said, any piece of information helps even if it doesn't seem that important. If it was them, though, it does seem strange that they'd be in a very popular vacation destination when they're actively missing, especially considering lots of Canadians go there.

Sofia: Yeah, that's weird, isn't it? The whole world pretty much knows who they are. I really hope it was them, because that means they're alive. Oh my gosh! I'm so sorry if that was rude of me. But then at least we'd know they're okay…well, maybe not okay mentally, but, like, physically.

Melissa: No worries, you weren't rude at all. You said exactly what I was thinking. It would also mean the police will track them down and bring them home sooner.

Sofia: Exactly, that's what we want! I don't mean to sound weird, but I already miss them being on the channel. I can't even imagine how you're feeling.

Melissa: I'm taking it one day at a time. That's all I can do right now. Once I talk to the police about this, they're probably going to want to speak to you as well. Would you be okay with that?

Sofia: Absolutely! Anything I can do to help.

Melissa: Okay, well I think that concludes today's video then. Thanks so much for your help, Sofia. It really means so much to me. If anyone else has any information they can pass along, please reach out to me, and I'll be in touch. Remember, we're offering a $5000 reward to anyone who knows where the kids are and can help us find them.

I do have another meeting with another potential lead tonight, so once I have more information, I will film another video and post it as soon as possible. Thanks for watching, and see you in the next video!

COMMENTS:

Kansas_Gurl: *Am I the only one who thinks this story sounds fake af?*

Taylor7765: *@Kansas_Gurl yeah that girl is totally lying. Probably just wanted to get on the channel and get her five minutes of fame :(*

Kansas_Gurl: *@Taylor7765 exactly!! Sad when three kids' lives are at risk, and all this girl cares about is getting famous!*

MikeR: *You could say the same thing about their so-called "mother."*

User454464349000: *Melissa, I SO appreciate you doing everything you can to get your kids back, but please don't let just anyone get on your channel. There are always going to be clout chasers out there, and sadly I think this girl is one of them. I promise this is no hate toward you, you've been doing such an amazing job! Just please be careful about people out there!*

xoxonatalie: *So sad this girl seems to be taking advantage of Melissa and her platform. Pete was such a great source of information, and I was hoping this girl would be, too. Hopefully there will be an update soon.*

CHAPTER 21

We've been walking for probably three hours now, and I'm starting to wonder if I have hypothermia.

Okay, maybe I'm being dramatic. I'm still wet, my teeth are chattering, and I'm beyond exhausted, but that doesn't mean I'm dying. I have no way of Googling my symptoms to be sure, which is probably a good thing; the last thing I need is something else to be anxious about. My body feels twice as heavy as I drag myself further into the forest. I'd love nothing more than to curl up and take a nap. It's probably been years since I last pulled an all-nighter, and judging by how sluggishly my siblings follow my lead, I assume this is their first time.

We've strayed from the shoreline, and I can faintly see the road in the distance. The woods have narrowed now, the shoreline just as far. We haven't had any luck finding a washed-up canoe or kayak, much to my disappointment, but it isn't exactly surprising. I don't know what I expected, really; a perfectly usable undamaged canoe appearing out of thin air to rescue us?

C'mon.

"We're almost there," Harper announces excitedly, gesturing up ahead. It's the third consecutive time she's stated the obvious, and I should be sharing her joy, but I'm *tired*. And scared.

"I know, Harper."

"But did you decide what we're doing? Are we knocking on the back door? Or are we—"

"Would you stop asking me that?" I snap. "The answer is the same as the last eighteen times you asked me. I. Don't. Know."

Shame overcomes me, and she puts me on blast before I can apologize. "'Kay, you don't have to take it out on me. I was just asking since we're about to be there. No need to be a bitch about it."

"Sorry. This night is just…it's a lot."

"Well, you're not the only one going through a hard time tonight. Don't forget about me and Levi."

It might be the exhaustion, but her statement strikes a nerve deep inside me. I see red. "Don't *forget* about you and Levi? Harper, all I've been doing all night is putting you two first, making sure you guys are safe, comforting you when you're scared. If I only cared about myself, I might've given up a long time ago. How can you say I've forgotten you with a straight face? Are you really that ungrateful? Maybe if you dig deep enough, you can find it in you to say thank you?"

Harper's jaw drops, and she seems to be stunned into silence at my outburst, because she doesn't respond. It doesn't stop me, though. "Do you think we'd be all the way out here, in the middle of nowhere, if I wasn't thinking about you? Do you think I wanted to sit through a thunderstorm, or sneak past bears, or get lost, or hurt my ankle? I want us *all* to go home, not just me. And I'm *trying*, okay? I'm trying the best that I can. Sorry it's not perfect, but there's no way it can be."

Harper's face crumples, and she bursts into tears. The sympathetic part of me feels like a bag of crap for making my sister cry, but a cruel part of me thinks, *good*. "I'm not ungrateful," she says between sobs. "I'm sorry. I just don't want Dad to kill us."

Her voice gives out before she finishes her sentence, her last few words a strangled whisper. Maybe I really am being too harsh, considering the possibility of Dad killing us is a very valid concern. God, why am I making being *thanked* a priority right now? I'm an asshole.

Levi joins Harper in the waterworks, sinking his face into her shoulder. "I don't want to die," he blubbers.

My lungs deflate, and I feel the sting of tears behind my own eyes. We're so close, yet so far from ending this nightmare. My brain is abuzz with worries and potential next steps, but I can't settle on one thought. We're running out of time, which is only adding to the mountain of pressure weighing me down. One thing is for sure; I can't give up. They can't do this alone.

I wrap my arms around both my siblings, squeezing them extra tight. It temporarily warms me up, and I don't want to let go. "I'm sorry," I tell them. "I didn't mean to snap like that. I'm just really stressed right now. We're going to get through this, okay? We just need to keep going for a little longer."

"And then what?" Harper says.

I don't know what happens next, but I'm not sure how to tell her. *There's a huge chance I'm going to screw this up? Maybe if we hope Dad gave up, that'll make it come true?* Instead, I settle on, "And then we knock on the door, unless we're rescued before then."

"How do we know that's going to work?"

I open my mouth to respond, but before I get the chance to say anything, a beam of white light flashes through the trees a few feet in front of us. My gaze darts toward the road, catching sight of the familiar car idling on the side of the road. A chill bolts down my spine.

It's Dad. And he's standing outside the car, pointing a flashlight into the forest.

"Oh no," I breathe. How did he know exactly where to stop? Does he see us?

I stand like a deer caught in the headlights, frozen in place. My instinct tells me to duck, but I can't move. *What do I do what do I do what do I do?*

"I know you're there," Dad calls out. "I just saw you. And I know you're probably freezing and would jump at the chance to sit inside a warm vehicle."

"Oh my God, Alyssa," Harper gasps, pulling Levi and I to the forest floor. Safe from his view, for now.

I press a finger to my lips. Any more talking will only make it easier for him to locate us.

"I know you're mad at me," Dad continues, "and I don't blame you. I messed up, bad. None of this was meant to scare you, and I'm sorry. I've made the decision to turn myself in."

I let his words sink in. It would be so easy to believe him, to feel the sensation of relief overtake me, to allow myself to accept a warm space and dry clothes. Every fibre of my being wants his words to be true. When tears spring to my eyes again, I let them fall this time, my body aching with want.

"You can trust me." Trees rustle as he makes his way into the forest. "Come with me into the car, and I'll bring us all to the police station. I'm realizing I went about this the wrong way, and this is the only way I can make it up to you. The police will take you back home, and your lives will go back to normal. You won't have to worry about me getting in your way anymore. Please, come on out."

It's over. Just go to him. Second by second, the fight leaves my body like a deflating balloon. I can't do this anymore. I'm cold, I'm tired, I'm sore, I'm starving, I'm scared, I'm angry, I'm—

"I know you can hear me. C'mon. You don't have to keep doing this. You're safe, I can promise you that."

I notice my hands are shaking, and I don't know whether it's from the cold or the fear. I've exhausted every option tonight, but I *tried*. I tried so fucking hard to do the right thing, but I've landed us right back at square one. I failed. He's getting closer, and if we try to run now, we'll probably be too late. The sky has slowly transitioned from its endless black to a deep shade of blue, and before long, we'll be fully exposed in the morning sunlight. I can't buy us anymore time.

The beam of the flashlight sweeps through the trees again. "You're all so strong, for everything you've gone through over the last few days. I'm so sorry. It's going to be okay now."

At the sound of his gentler tone, I'm transported back to my childhood bedroom, when the same voice would read me bedtime stories late into the night, never hesitating when I begged for "just one more." The same voice that told me I was going to be a big sister, that assured me just because there was a new baby at home, it didn't mean he and Mom loved me less. The same voice that consoled me on my first day of kindergarten when I threw a tantrum in the parking lot because I didn't want to go. I try to imagine the voice I'm hearing now belongs to the same man, but it's impossible when I've now stared down the barrel of his gun. The betrayal stings more than I ever could have imagined.

Should I keep fighting for us, or forgive and move on? Does he deserve a second chance?

Maybe we should end this once and for all. I won't let the gun scare me this time.

I start to pull myself to my feet, but Harper's hand clamps around my wrist just as quickly, yanking me back down. "Are you crazy?" she whispers. "What the hell are you doing? He's going to see you."

"We should go." Tears blur my vision. "End this now. He'll take us home."

She shakes her head vigorously. "No, Alyssa. The whole point of this night was to make it out ourselves. You've been saying all night not to trust him, and now all of a sudden you do? What's wrong with you?"

I do trust him. I don't trust him. All I'm seeing is an easy way out.

"You worked hard for this, Alyssa. Don't. Please."

My heart unexpectedly warms at her acknowledgement of everything I've done tonight. I'm not exactly looking to be hailed as a hero, but it feels good to be seen. Ahead of me, Dad combs through the brush, threatening to destroy all my hard work with each step.

"Are you really going to pass up this opportunity?" Dad's tone has darkened. "All I'm trying to do is help you. Do you think I'd be all the way out here looking for you if I wanted to harm you?"

Snap. More branches break beneath his weight. In the distance, a coyote howls.

"I'm not trying to make this all about me, nor all about your mom. It might seem that way, but I promise, everything I do is for you three. So you can take the offer, or you can leave it. But while I have your attention, I thought I'd let you know that your mom has just been reported missing. I was hoping you could help me find her."

FOR IMMEDIATE RELEASE
JULY 1, 2024

Mother of Abducted "BennettFam" Children Has Gone Missing

SAWYER, ON—The mother of abducted YouTube stars Alyssa, Harper, and Levi Bennett, who disappeared earlier this week from their Sawyer residence, has been reported missing.

Melissa Bennett, 35, of Sawyer, was last seen attending a search party for her three missing children in the Main Street area earlier this afternoon. Bennett's children were abducted from their Tower Drive residence at gunpoint on June 30th by their father, Daniel Bennett, 35, of Toronto. Her purse, phone, and vehicle were found at her home this evening. There is concern for her safety, and it is determined that the two incidents are likely connected. Her disappearance is being treated as suspicious.

Bennett is described as being 5'5, 120lbs with long brunette hair with blond highlights, and was last seen wearing a black "grow through what you go through" t-shirt with white flowers, blue jeans, and white Nike sneakers.

Bennett, known for her popular family YouTube channel "TheBennettFam," had most recently been posting videos to her channel to spread awareness of her children's disappearance to her 4.3 million subscribers. Her last two videos, in which she interviewed people with potential information on the case, have amassed over 5 million combined views, and police are looking to speak with all involved parties. At this time, there is no threat to public safety. Anyone with information regarding Bennett's disappearance is encouraged to come forward and speak with the Sawyer Regional Police Department immediately.

PRESS RELEASE COMMENTS:

Sarahhh545: *I KNEW there was something weird about that last video. I really hope everyone is found safe and sound :(*
sawyerlocal: *That sick man definitely kidnapped her, too. There's absolutely no way these 2 incidents aren't related.*
Suez365: *Melissa would NEVER just run away, especially with how hard she's been working to try and find her kids! She wouldn't just give up on them. Dan did something to her. This story has my stomach in knots, and I'm really praying for a positive outcome.*
GagneFarah: *I still feel like this has to be a publicity stunt. Sorry to say it, but that woman is soooo narcissistic. She'll do anything for the views. And more views = more money.*

CHAPTER 22

The bottom drops out of my world, and everything is spinning, spinning, until I'm brought back down to my knees. No. *No no no no.*

"I wanted to contact her first, let her know I was going to bring you three home," Dad says now, his voice filtering through the noise in my head. "Then I saw the article. She went missing while searching for you."

My stomach lurches. I want to believe he's lying, but his tone tells me otherwise. He sounds almost excited to be announcing this to us, as if it's the newest piece of gossip he's been dying to spill. I choke on a sob as he continues. "It was a huge search party that all her subscribers knew about. My gut tells me some crazy obsessed fan probably travelled there to meet up with her and took matters into his own hands."

Somehow, I feel responsible for this, even though I have no idea what happened to her. Maybe if I'd somehow prevented our kidnapping, she wouldn't have been out there searching for us in the first place, putting herself in harm's way. I know, without a doubt, that Dad did this to her. Whether or not she's alive is the bigger question.

Please let her be okay. Dear God, don't let her die.

I was so close to letting my siblings and I get into his car just a few moments ago, and nausea overtakes me at the thought. How could I be so naïve? How could he promise to take us home when Mom isn't even there? Where is he really planning to take us if he manages to catch us? And, most importantly, what has he done to Mom?

There's no way he doesn't know he'll be the top suspect, even if he didn't kidnap her. No one will buy the story that she just disappeared a day after her kids were taken by their father. There's a clear motive— Mom's video about the divorce—which should hopefully mean the cops are getting closer to finding him. The most likely scenario I can think of is that Mom gave the cops tons of information that could point to our whereabouts, and Dad needed her to keep quiet, so he kidnapped her, too. But how could he have done it without being seen in Sawyer?

My mouth goes dry. There are so many possibilities, but none of them make sense to me.

"Rumour has it your mother was making YouTube videos interviewing random people to try and find you guys." Dad barks a laugh, and it echoes in the still night air. "Doesn't surprise me, though, considering that channel is everything to her. Gotta capitalize off your missing children, right?"

He's to the far right of us now, and as I watch him travel in the wrong direction, I realize we still have a chance to get out of here without being seen. I suddenly get an idea, one so crazy and unrealistic it has me questioning my sanity. We might not need to steal a boat or knock on anyone's door. If I can pull this off, it'll be a total miracle, but if I don't, we might be in some serious trouble. We have to try, anyway.

I wait until he's walked a few more feet, then I gesture for Harper and Levi to get up. "That way." I gesture left, toward the road. "Quietly."

Levi draws his knees to chest. "What if he finds us?"

I shake my head gesture for them to follow. Reluctantly, Harper and Levi crawl after me as we make our way toward the road. Dad shouldn't be able to hear us with how slow we're moving, and he shouldn't see us as long as we don't stand yet. I briefly reconsider whether or not I want to voice my new plan, but ultimately I decide it's better than no plan at all. Once we commit, there's no turning back.

I pull a small rock from the damp earth beneath me and run my thumb along its surface. It serves as a temporary comfort and a welcome distraction from the events that have unfolded tonight. Clutching it tightly, I draw a deep breath in and exhale a rushed rehearsal of what we're going to do next. "We have to distract him so he thinks we're further into the bush than we are. Maybe we start throwing some rocks or sticks as far away as we can so he hears the noise. Then once he follows, we're going to steal the car."

CHAPTER 23

There are a million ways this could go wrong. It doesn't take a genius to figure that one out.

For starters, he might not have even left the keys in the car. If that's the case, then we're truly screwed. I think I hear the car running, but that could be my imagination playing tricks on me; I can't count on it yet.

Secondly, we might not be fast enough. From the point in the forest we decide to start running, we have to make it to the car, pile inside, and drive off all within the span of a few seconds to ensure he doesn't catch up.

And—the thought that tangles my stomach in knots—we have to make the distractions work. The more I think about it, the more childish it sounds. When the rocks and sticks hit the ground, is he really going to follow the sounds like a lost puppy? There's also a chance he sees us throwing the objects, in which case it'd be game over.

Or he decides to give up and head back to the car before we start.

The footsteps crunch closer. *Oh God, oh God.*

"Alyssa, are you freaking crazy? We can't—" Harper starts, but I cut her off.

"Trust me." *Jesus Christ, stop talking. He's going to hear us.*

We'll drive to the closest town and find someone to call the police. Then it'll be all over. If we stay quiet, we should be able to execute this plan the way I want.

Harper and Levi both stare back at me wide-eyed, as if I have three heads. I press a finger to my lips and use my other hand to throw the rock as far away from us as possible. The rock is too small, and the impact barely makes a noise. I scramble around the forest floor in search of more, and my hands eventually close around a much larger rock. "Don't just stand there," I hiss, and Levi's face crumples. He scoops up a stick with shaking hands and tosses it in the same direction I threw the rock.

When the larger rock hits the ground, it captures Dad's attention. He snaps his head up, and his gaze follows the echo. "Are you guys okay over there? Is someone hurt?"

My lungs constrict as the beam of the flashlight sweeps too close to us, and I flatten myself against the ground, wishing I could sink beneath it and disappear entirely. "I know where you are," he warns, "and if you're trying to mess with me, it's not working. I'm not stupid."

I bristle. Harper and Levi crouch next to me, and we lie in total silence as his footsteps draw nearer. He's on to us, and rather than giving us a head start, I think I've just made things so much worse. He must've seen me throw the rock. I press my forehead against the cool dirt and take a few deep breaths, which do nothing to calm my racing heart. Wherever Mom is, we might be joining her if I don't find us a way out of here.

I'm so sorry, Mom. I'm trying. I'm trying like hell to save you. I can't let my brain convince me she's dead. Not after everything she's gone through over the last couple days. We're going to get in the car, get some help, and the police will find her safe and sound shortly after. She could be locked away in a basement somewhere, cut off from the world, scrambling to escape just like we were. I need to try harder to reach her; after everything she's done for us, it's the least I can do.

As much as Dad hates her and everything she stands for, she doesn't deserve this. She sounds like she's been using her channel to her advantage to try and find us, which I have to admire. Social media isn't all bad, right?

I sneak a glance toward Dad, and much to my relief, he begins to comb his way through the trees in the direction of the rock. I wait until he's turned his back to us to proceed, and I hold my breath as we crawl, knowing he could turn back to the car at any given moment. Do I throw something else? Do I move faster? Like every other plan I've had tonight, there is no backup in case something goes wrong, and if I keep reminding myself of that fact, I'll probably back out. There's no time to second guess anything; I have to act now.

Before I know it, there's another rock in my hand, and I'm hurling it toward Dad. I don't watch where it lands, but I hear his grunt of disapproval; or fear, maybe, that there's an animal lurking nearby. "I know you're there," he says. "And I know you're scared. Please, come with me."

I want to scream, *why would we come with you? If Mom is missing, where are you going to bring us? Surely not home?*

That's when my knee comes down on a large branch, and the following snap is like an explosion in the dead silence.

I inhale sharply, gritting my teeth. It's not easy to move quietly out here, especially when I know Dad is listening. Behind me, more footsteps sound in the still night. "Alyssa? Was that you?"

I risk another peek over my shoulder to check the distance between us and lock eyes with my father.

The blood drains from my face.

Shit. Oh shit. Oh my God.

He acts immediately, breaking out into a sprint through the brush, and I grab a fistful of Levi's hoodie, yanking him upright. "Go! We need to go!" I scream, and Harper frantically gets to her feet, only to stumble and catch herself against a tree trunk. My hand closes around her arm, and I drag her after me. "Run!"

"I'm not here to hurt you, goddammit!" Dad roars after us. "Would you stop being so dramatic and listen to me for five minutes?"

But I'm not listening. Just as I did earlier tonight, I run with all the strength I have left in me, eyeing the BMW up ahead. Panic claws at me, seizing my lungs, clouding my vision. I messed up big time, and I mentally kick myself. How could I be so stupid to look back?

Now I'm absolutely certain there is nothing Dad can say to me that can change my mind. We've reached the point of no return, and I pray like hell the doors are unlocked, and the key is inside. I pump my legs harder, willing them to move faster, and my sore ankle throbs in response, shooting electric jolts of pain through my foot. *Almost there. Don't stop now. You're almost there.*

Five hundred feet to safety. Harper, ever the track star, pulls her arm out of my grip and dashes ahead of us, shoving branches out of the way to make a temporary clearing for us. Her ponytail sways behind her, and one of the pant legs of her jumpsuit snags in a branch, tearing the fabric, but she never falters.

One hundred feet to safety. The crunch of dad's shoes are thunderous drum beats as they approach, thrumming in my ears. He's more than determined to catch us, and though it's three against one, I know exactly what his thoughts are; if he catches only me, who's going to drive to get us help? Certainly not my siblings. That's why I have to make this work.

Twenty feet to safety. The road beckons us, and Harper crosses the threshold first, making a beeline for the BMW. The lights are on, the small cloud of exhaust confirming the best news possible; the engine is already idling. The feel of the dirt road beneath my feet is a welcome relief. We're going home tonight.

"Hey!" Dad cries as Harper circles around to the passenger door. "Don't you dare! Don't you *fucking* dare!"

Harper tugs on the door handle, again and again, but the door doesn't budge. The flicker of hope burns out in my chest just as quickly as it ignited.

It's locked.

But wait. The driver's side might be unlocked.

Harper lets out a half scream, half cry. "It's not opening!"

Levi and I reach the car with Dad hot on our heels. I yank the handle, and the door miraculously pops open. I don't have time to be relieved yet. With shaking fingers, I press the button to unlock the passenger doors, and the following *click* is music to my ears. "Get in!" I shout, and Harper and Levi dive inside, barely closing their doors before I slam the car into gear and stomp on the gas.

Dad's fist pounds against the door behind me—Levi's door—for one second, but it's too late; we're off. The engine roars in response, and the car flies down the quiet road, leaving Dad stranded on the road in the middle of nowhere.

My laugh comes out of nowhere, but now that I've started, I can't stop. It takes over my whole body, and as I fumble with my seatbelt, Harper joins in, slapping her thigh. "Oh my God, Alyssa! You did it!"

"*We* did it," I correct her between giggles.

"But you planned it," Levi adds.

"I can't believe that actually worked. That was straight out of a movie scene. You know I can't take the full credit." I glance at both of them quickly. "Make sure your seatbelts are on, by the way."

I hear them click into place. "Well, because of you, we get to go home," Harper says, bursting into another fit of laughter. "And now Dad is getting a taste of his own medicine."

I smirk. "That was the goal. What do you say we stop at McDonald's once this is over and done with?"

CHAPTER 24

My knuckles are white on the steering wheel as I navigate the quiet road, my gaze darting left and right to watch for wildlife. Despite any hard feelings I have for Dad, the pressure to keep this car in immaculate condition weighs heavy on my shoulders. He'd be livid if I dented it or scratched the rims, as I would be if it was my own car. I shouldn't care, considering jail will prevent him from driving it or even seeing it, but for some reason I do. It's the first time I've ever driven it.

The sun is almost above the horizon, painting the sky a lovely combination of orange and red. I admire it for just a few seconds before I focus on the next task; get to the highway and drive until the next town. From what I remember, all I need to do is keep driving straight, then I'll see it.

"Did Dad leave any phones in here?" I ask my siblings. "We can call the police if we have a signal."

Harper opens the glove compartment, and I feel Levi check the pocket behind my seat. When they both report that there aren't any, disappointment fills my chest, but only for a second. We're still going to get to safety, no matter how long it takes to get there. There weren't many towns in the direction we came from, so if I head in the opposite direction and turn right instead of left, maybe we'll find a closer town. There's a chance we get pulled over by the police anyway if another motorist recognizes the license plate and calls them. My heart gallops as I imagine what it will feel like to finally be rescued. *Soon. Just keep driving.*

I steal a glimpse at the gas gauge; a little over a quarter tank. Not ideal, but we should be fine. It's better than being on foot, that's for sure.

"I still can't believe I pulled that off," I breathe. My damp hoodie clings to my body, and I finally have the luxury of heat. I crank it, and there's a collective sigh of relief throughout the car. "Was that even real? Am I dreaming?"

"Nope, it really happened." Harper smiles. "You should have seen the look on Dad's face when we drove away. I wish we had a replay button! He was looking at us like he couldn't believe we had the *audacity* to think about taking the car. Like, not our fault you're stupid and left the keys in it."

"The nerve of us, right? He practically invited us to take it!"

"First you stick us in a basement that has a window. Next you leave your car running when you know your hostages are nearby. Not so good at this whole kidnapping thing, are you?"

"Better luck next time, I guess!"

Harper hollers with laughter and pretends to hold a phone in front of her face. *"Hi Bennett FamJams, this is Dan Bennett here, reporting live from prison!"*

"I didn't read enough books about how to kidnap someone, so here I am in a complete change of scenery! Guess I'd better get used to it."

This gets Levi laughing, too. It feels good to have the three of us sharing a moment of joy again, and it's something I promise to never take for granted. These past few days have given me a greater appreciation for the small things, from the smell of rain to simply joking around with my siblings. Even the big things—the house, my car, my entire privileged life—deserve the proper recognition, and now I can't believe I used to resent it all. Our YouTube channel may have taken some things from us, like our privacy, but it's also given us more than we could have ever dreamed of. Not everyone gets so lucky.

Though, we definitely need to have a discussion with Mom about the future of the channel when we get home. Maybe this whole thing can serve as a wake-up call and allow for some boundaries to be put in place. Of course, it can wait until we've had some time to process the traumas of this weekend, but it can't be avoided forever. For now, all I want to do is hold everyone in my family a little tighter and soak in all the extra time we'll have together this summer.

"There's the cottage we were supposed to go to," Harper says, snapping me out of my daze.

I look ahead, and sure enough, we're about to approach the three cottages we were walking to. Turns out we didn't have much further to go on foot, but I have to pat myself on the back for hijacking the car; with how exhausted my body is, I can't even begin to imagine what the rest of the walk would've felt like. At least we've saved ourselves some time.

The trees conceal some of the driveways, so by the time I see the car pulling out, it's too late.

A silver Toyota Corolla peels down the driveway at an unusually quick speed, and I barely have the time to react. My foot slams on the brakes as a gasp escapes my lips, the sound of grinding gravel filling my eardrums. Everything seems to happen in slow motion; the front end of the BMW slamming into the passenger door of the Corolla, the force throwing my body forward, the seatbelt digging into my skin. My forehead collides with the steering wheel, and a burst of pain travels through me. The crunch of metal on metal seems to linger, echoing in my head. *Oh God. We're done. Oh God. Oh God.*

I crashed the car. I crashed the stupid car and it's all my fault and we're all probably hurt and I wrecked someone else's car but why the fuck were they driving down the driveway so fast in the first place?

I frantically look around the BMW for my siblings, my skull pounding. "Oh my God. Are you guys okay? Are you hurt? I'm so sorry. I'm so, so, so sorry."

Levi bursts into tears, and Harper rubs the back of her neck. "I'm fine," she croaks. "But what are we gonna—?"

"Levi, you didn't answer me. Are you okay?"

He hesitates before gulping out a "Yep." Good. Now I need to check on the other driver.

I unbuckle my seatbelt and step out, ignoring the flares of pain that shoot through my body as I run around to the other side of the Corolla. A man is climbing out, his eyes wide like he can't believe what just happened. "I'm so sorry, sir! I didn't see you coming and everything happened so fast and just…are you okay?"

He stretches his arms above his head and tilts his neck to the side, groaning slightly. "A little sore, but I'm all right. What about you? You shouldn't be driving down this road so fast, especially this early in the morning."

"Sorry. I'm fine." What I really want to do is grab this man by his stupid shoulders and shake him. I'm pretty sure I was going the speed limit. Who the hell does he think he is accusing *me* of going too fast when he was the one who whipped out of the driveway like he was a NASCAR driver? Now our plans are totally ruined.

I force a deep breath through my lungs. Everyone's okay. That's all that matters.

We're still going to get out of here. Now all I have to do is trauma dump on this poor man and make him call the police for us.

Will he even believe what I'm about to say? This is humiliating. "Um, sir, we actually need your help with something. We've—"

"We can't just leave our cars in the road," he interrupts. "We're going to have to call a tow truck." He gestures behind him to the totaled cars. "And, obviously, get our insurance stuff sorted."

Guilt gnaws at my stomach. "I'm really sorry about your car. I didn't mean to wreck it." I instinctively check over my shoulder to see if Dad has caught up to us. He hasn't. "But we really need your help. We were kidnapped by our dad a couple days ago and there's an Amber Alert out for us right now. We're the Bennetts. My name is Alyssa, and my siblings Harper and Levi are sitting in the car. We just escaped, and that's his car we were driving. We need you to call the police for us, and I promise we'll sort out the insurance thing after, but he's coming back for us any minute and I don't want to get caught. Please. Can you just do that for us?"

He furrows his brows and scratches the back of his neck. There's confusion written all over his face. He definitely doesn't believe us. "You can Google it," I add. "I'm pretty sure it's all over the internet, but we have a YouTube channel and—"

"No, I remember you." His eyes light up. "Oh my God. You're those kids that were abducted out of Sawyer. TheBennettFam. Your dad showed up at your door with a gun and took you."

"Yes!" My eyes well in relief. "That's us. He's coming up the road, and he's looking for us. We don't have any phones on us. Can you call the police, like, right now?"

"Yeah, yeah, I left my phone in the house, though. Wow, I can't believe it's really you. Let me just back the car into the driveway real quick and I'll go get the phone."

As he climbs back into the Corolla, I quickly jump into the BMW to pull onto the shoulder of the road. Miraculously, the car is still running despite the massive cave in the front end. "So, is he calling the police or what?" Harper asks, drawing her knees to her chest.

I nod. "He just wanted us to get our cars out of the road first. Come on, let's get out and wait for the police with him. That way, if Dad manages to show up, this guy will protect us."

I throw the car in park and step back out, Harper and Levi following behind. As we cross the street toward our old cottage, the man greets us at the end of the driveway, waving us over. "You'd better come inside until the police get here," he tells us. "You guys can warm up a bit while I call them."

"Awesome." I take a quick look around the yard. I haven't been here in years, and nostalgia hits me as I catch sight of the sunrise over the water. As a kid, I'd beg Mom and Dad to go outside the moment I saw a sliver of sunlight over the lake, and they'd reluctantly agree, as long as I'd eaten breakfast first. Harper and I played outside every chance we got, and once Levi was born, we'd lay him on a picnic blanket in the grass and keep him occupied while Mom and Dad relaxed on the porch. We were often joined by the kids next door, and as my gaze turns to the cottages on either side of us, I notice both driveways are empty. It's only the second day of summer vacation; maybe the families don't have plans to come out here just yet. For now, we're completely alone with this man.

My pulse spikes a little as it dawns on me. I don't want to let it bother me, but to err on the side of caution, maybe we should wait outside until the police come here. I can't seem to let go of the paranoia after being locked in a basement for the past two days, and besides, it might be nice to hang out in the backyard again like old times. Dad won't see us back here; the police will likely beat him here.

"I think we'll just wait outside instead, but thank you for the offer." I gesture to the lake. "This actually used to be our old cottage when we were little, and I kind of want to check out the yard again. We could probably use the fresh air, anyway."

He dismisses me with a wave. "No, I insist. You just had hours of 'fresh air.' You need to warm up."

"Yeah, I'm freezing." Harper shivers for extra effect. "I don't want to stand outside."

I shoot Harper a look. "It won't be for long. I just want to look around for a bit."

"Actually, I think you should really come inside." When my gaze returns to the man, the air around me stills as I catch sight of his gun, pointed directly at me. He uses his other hand to open the side door, and when his next words come, I hear them as if they're being spoken to me underwater. "I have a nice surprise waiting for you. Trust me, you won't want to miss it."

CHAPTER 25

I'm frozen to the spot. Harper and Levi's combined screams sound behind me, but I barely hear them over the rush of blood in my ears. They both run through the open door, but I can't seem to make my feet move.

The man's blond eyebrows knit together, and his face contorts with anger. "Let me repeat myself, in case you didn't understand the first time," he spits. "Get. Inside. The. House."

Slowly, my feet start to move, but they don't feel like my own. This man is completely different to the person I spoke to a few minutes ago; the gentle demeanor is gone, replaced with a steel gaze that could burn a hole right through me. All night, I've been telling myself to trust no one; how could I have let my guard down so easily? I should've just taken the risk and kept driving. I should've known it was a trap.

I force myself up the few steps to the kitchen. They haven't changed the cottage much since my parents sold it; the wood paneling and white floor have remained untouched, but there's a few floral canvases hanging on the walls. The kitchen countertops are bare, scrubbed clean, and there's a broom propped up in the corner. There's no evidence of anyone staying here; it's as if the place has been staged for a showing.

I turn right to head to the living room, and that's when I lock eyes with my mother.

A gasp rips its way through my chest, startling me. Her eyes widen, and she tries to get up, but her hands and feet are tied to the chair she sits in. *She's alive. Thank God, she's alive.* "Mom!" Harper and Levi shriek in unison, but before they can run to her, the man yells at them to stay where they are.

"This isn't going to be some cute little reunion," he tells us, venom coating his words. "I'll let you get your last words in with her, but make it quick. She's got about—" he makes a show of checking his watch—"twenty or thirty minutes left to live, depending on how generous I'm feeling."

"Don't you dare touch her," I growl. "Whatever she did wrong, we can fix it without killing her."

Tears track down Mom's cheeks, her features sagging in defeat. "Don't do this in front of my kids, Pete. Please. They didn't do anything wrong."

Pete. Of course this is Pete. I'm finally face to face with the man I've heard so much about, the man whose cottage we've been trapped in, the man my father confessed to regretting us to. Of course they were working together; I've known that all along. The bigger question is why? Why would Pete care enough about Dad's life, about our lives, enough to want to kill my mother and carry out a kidnapping plot?

When I see the dark bruise on Mom's cheek, I see red. I lunge at Pete, but he shoves me back effortlessly, sending me toppling to the floor. "Nice try, honey," he laughs. "Pretty daring, though, I have to admit. Trying to attack the guy with a loaded gun."

"Leave her alone!" I yell. I scramble back to my feet, and he aims the gun at me once again. "You're not going to shoot me. You're just trying to scare me."

"I will if you try and help her out of here. I won't kill you, but the pain will be bad enough that you'll wish I did."

"Why are you so obsessed with my family? You're a psychopath!"

"It's okay, Alyssa," Mom whimpers. "Don't—"

"It's *not* okay." My voice wobbles, and I fight to keep it steady. "We're not growing up without a mother because some guy who doesn't even know you decided you deserve to die. There are two sides to every story. His side isn't the only one that matters."

"I know, baby. Just let me handle it."

The side door swings open, and Dad walks in, his hair disheveled and his skin damp with sweat. When he sees Harper, Levi and I huddled together in the living room, he smirks. "Thought I'd find you guys here. Didn't get very far, did you?"

I never thought it was possible to hate someone so much, but in this moment, I wish he was dead. My blood boils as he walks straight by us, lowering himself onto the couch next to Mom's chair and tucking a strand of her hair behind her ear. "You really have to admire their determination, though. They broke a window, ran through the woods for hours, stole my car *and* survived crashing it. If I didn't call Pete to give him a heads up that they were coming down the road, he might not have stopped them in time, and they'd have gotten away."

Mom whimpers, and Dad shushes her. "They really are attached to you for some reason. They're probably just brainwashed after everything you've done to them. It's too bad you couldn't have changed your ways sooner, otherwise I might have let you live, but you just don't listen. You had your chance. The kids don't want to stay with me, but they won't have a choice after today."

"They're going to catch you, you know," I snarl. "If you think you can get away with killing her, you have it all wrong. You don't even know how to hold someone hostage properly, otherwise we wouldn't have escaped. You really think the police won't find you if you kill her?"

"That's not your problem to worry about."

"You don't have any confidence. You're pretending you do, but you really don't."

"Good thing I'm here to help then, right?" Pete chuckles, waving the gun back and forth. "As far as your little fans are aware, I'm just trying to help a friend find her missing children. They think your dad wanted to take you to Mexico, so everyone seems to be focusing their attention on finding you there. The power of influence, right? If someone said it on the internet, then it must be true."

I glare at him. "Fuck you."

"I have to admit, though, your mother would do anything to find you. I guess it's the only time she's actually appreciated you, other than forcing you to give her content. All I had to do was tell her I had more information on you, that she needed to meet me at this cottage, and she showed up quickly. But how are we supposed to trust that she's not going to take you home and keep exploiting your lives?"

"We can't," Dad adds. "Which is why we have to do this."

"I don't understand any of this." My voice is almost a whine. I drop down onto the opposite couch and take hold of my siblings' hands. "This has clearly been planned for months. It wasn't just because of one video Mom made talking about the divorce. Pete has obviously been involved this whole time, so why is he bothering to help you?"

"Well, we can start from the beginning. We've worked together for almost your whole life, and he's been the only person I can open up to about our circumstances. He knows how tough it's been for me, so he wanted to help, because he's a good friend of mine who would do anything for me. He bought this cottage after us, and now owns the two next door, and the one we just stayed in. He rents them out to campers. Luckily, that has been giving us places to stay until we can follow through with the next plan of leaving the country. Not to Mexico, though. I'm leaving it a surprise for now."

Pete nods along, pacing the floor in front of us. "Think of the divorce video as the straw that broke the camel's back. We planned to do this soon, but not this soon. After that video, he realized you three weren't safe under her roof anymore."

"That's such bullshit." I throw my hands in the air. "How were we not safe? We had a roof over our heads, food, and basically anything we wanted. It's a little dramatic to claim we weren't safe."

"Come on, Alyssa, you know exactly what we mean. Don't play stupid. You know your family has had stalkers before. Weird, obsessed fans who easily could have hurt you."

He does have a point, admittedly. "Okay, but no one ever did hurt us. I don't feel safe with my dad, especially with both of you waving guns in our faces, threatening us."

"Lissy, I'm going to tell you something about the channel, and you're not going to like it." Dad swallows hard. "You don't have back-end access to the channel like your mom does. You don't see the channel's analytics, other than your video views and subscriber count. Every day, I had to go in to the channel and check those analytics, and make sure they weren't somehow wrong. Lissy, the highest number of viewers and engagement are from men between the ages of 45 and 54."

Darkness overtakes the corners of my vision, and the room tilts. No. No, that can't be right. "But…well…they're just supposed to be fun videos about our lives," I protest weakly. "Anyone can like them."

"Lissy, I know this is hard to hear, but there's no way you can justify this. You know as well as anyone that that's not your target demographic. Sure, men between those ages *can* like your videos. But right now, they're your biggest audience. There's something wrong with that."

I sink my head into my hands, fighting the urge to throw up. "So you're saying…we have *pedophiles* watching our videos?"

"Yes. You probably do. And if you take a look at the most viral videos on the channel, what are they about? Mostly clothing try-on hauls, from you. Pool party videos. Videos that should never capture the attention of that demographic."

My body tingles all over, and I worry I'm going to pass out. Mom would have known this all along; she was obsessed with the channel's numbers, always looking for ways to make the channel grow. And she didn't do anything but keep making videos. 95 percent of the video ideas came from her.

Without warning, I start to dry heave. Harper starts to cry and yells, "That's so messed up! What the hell?"

"I know it is." Dad clasps his hands together. "So, do you see now why it was unsafe to keep you there? Your mom knew all along, but did nothing about it. She knew the kind of money that would come from those videos, so she filmed and posted lots of them."

Mom has stayed silent the entire time Dad has been talking, and when I finally lift my head to look at her, she pales, avoiding eye contact. Guilty as sin. I knew she'd do anything for content, but I never imagined she'd stoop this low. Now I'm caught in the middle all over again, wondering which parent we'll be safer with.

None of them, from the sounds of it. But what do we do now?

I look at Mom across the room, but she avoids my gaze. "Mom, is this true?" I ask around the lump in my throat.

I desperately want her to tell me they're lying, but she squeezes her eyes shut and doesn't say anything.

"*Mom.* Answer me."

She hangs her head and nods slowly, letting a few tears leak out. Guilty. "I'm sorry," she whispers. "I know you probably think I'm a terrible mother. I really have tried to give you guys the best lives possible, but this was far from the right way to do it. I'm so, so sorry."

"How could you do that to us?"

Mom starts to speak, but Pete interrupts. "To make things fair for everyone, we'll give her the chance to explain her side of the story. But at the end of the day, she needs to pay for everything she's done. Keep talking, but no matter what you say, we're still going to kill you after."

Mom gulps. "Okay."

CHAPTER 26

"Go on," Dad urges.

Mom sighs heavily, allowing the tears to flow freely down her cheeks as she turns her attention toward us. "None of what I'm about to say is an excuse for posting videos of you every day, knowing what kind of audience we had. I guess a part of me wanted to believe it wasn't true, or that it was exaggerated, but data doesn't lie. I was hoping it was just a one-time stat, that it would go away after we posted more videos, which I'm realizing now is incredibly stupid to think."

"It made you money, which was the only thing you cared about."

"This is supposed to be *my* time to talk, remember?" Mom glares at Dad, and he throws his hands in the air. "So, let me say what I need to say, then you can move forward with your little plan."

"Got it. Keep talking, then."

"I never started the YouTube channel with the intention to get famous. At the time, I didn't even know you could make money from it, and turn it into a career. It wasn't popular for that back then. I've told you before that I started it as a pregnant teenager just trying to find a community with other teen moms, considering I barely had any support from friends or family. Everyone told me having a baby that young would ruin my life. I wanted to help other teen moms who had been told the same thing feel less alone, so I started making videos to show them it's still possible to give your kids a good life, but also be transparent by showing the good and the bad. I obviously didn't want to encourage teen pregnancy."

It's a story I've heard a million times, a story that was constantly shared with our audience. It's also a story that was sometimes used against us if we didn't want to be in a video: *I'm doing this for you. You should be grateful this little hobby turned into a career that supports you. Not everyone gets this opportunity.*

"Then one day, the channel just...blew up. People said they loved how authentic my videos were, and next thing I knew, companies were offering to sponsor me. Before, I was so stressed about how I was going to balance both college and raising a baby, but the more money that came in, the more I realized I didn't need college when *this* could be my job. People started requesting daily vlogs, and it was so cool knowing there were people who wanted to see my daily life. I never thought I could be that interesting. So their opinions started to become...kind of like an addiction."

"*Kind* of like an addiction," Dad snorts. Mom shoots him a look, and he scoffs. "Sorry. Go on."

"I don't need to tell you that 4.3 million is a lot, and while I'm really proud of myself for getting there, I couldn't have done it without my kids." She smiles weakly. "I wouldn't have this life if it wasn't for you, but I never thought it'd come at the cost of your privacy. I got lost in those big numbers, and I can't tell you enough how sorry I am for that. I used you for content. That's awful."

Harper, Levi and I exchange glances. It's the apology we've been waiting forever for, but I don't feel any better. I don't know if she deserves forgiveness yet, but she also doesn't deserve to die. Part of me wonders if the apology is genuine in the first place; maybe she's just saying this in the hopes Dad will change his mind. I just want to go home and forget these last few days ever happened. Once again, we're caught in the middle of our parents' drama, expected to pick a side. I'm sick of it.

"I didn't acknowledge how much it harmed you," Mom continues. "I thought having lots of money and everything it could buy would be enough, but I ignored that you were being bullied, and that you became public figures without your consent. I was obviously too addicted to social media, and should've listened when you said you didn't want to be filmed. You were right; certain things should've been kept private, like getting your period or wetting the bed. I wanted to help others so badly I was ignoring my own kids."

"Thank you." The words surprise me when I utter them, and her eyes light up a little. I direct my attention back to Dad. "There. She's said what she needed to say. Can we go home now?"

Dad purses his lips, pretending to be lost in thought. "Well, it was a good enough apology, but she glossed over a couple of the other issues. Like the fact that people used to write Wattpad fanfictions about you three, which is quite frankly a little disturbing. Or the couple

146

people on TikTok who used to use pictures and videos of you three, pretending you were their kids. Your mom knew all that was happening, but did she reach out to those creators and make them take the content down? Just ask her."

I swallow another wave of nausea. "So she messed up and admitted it, okay? But you don't need to kill her. What happened to your whole speech about turning yourself in? Guess you lied like you always do."

"Yeah, we almost fell for it," says Harper. "Maybe you're lying about everything you've just said about the channel."

"I wish I was, sweetie." Dad folds his arms across his chest. "I wouldn't do all this for nothing. I've given your mom so many chances to make this right, and she's failed every time. That's why we have to kill her; it's the only way to make sure she never hurts you again."

I shake my head. "You're not a killer, Dad. Admit it. You've never hurt anyone like this in your life. I don't think you're capable, if I'm being honest."

"Like Pete said earlier, that's why he's here to help."

Pete raises his gun at Mom again, his finger moving quickly to the trigger. Mom inhales sharply, tears springing back to her eyes. "Any last words before you go?"

A strangled sob escapes Mom's lips. Her body convulses against the restraints, so hard I worry she's going to topple the chair over. "You don't want to do this. I've said I'm sorry. Please, there has to be something else I can do. My kids need me."

It's the first time since we got here that I've seen her beg for her life. It's exactly what they want, and she's fallen right into their trap. The desperation to help her floods my chest, but if I get up, Pete will shoot me too.

"Your kids have needed you all this time, Melissa, and you weren't there for them like you should've been. Oh, the consequences of your own actions. Never thought you'd actually be held accountable, huh?"

"Please! It'll be different this time, I swear. The first thing I'll do when I get home is delete that channel and never make another video again. If you'd just give me—"

Dad barks out a laugh. "Heard that one before. Some things just don't change."

Pete smiles. "Well, I guess we should take care of this, then."

I flinch and squeeze my eyes shut, panic bubbling in my chest. They're actually going to do it. There's nothing I can do to save her now. "No, Mom!" Levi yells, piercing my eardrums.

I'm about to lose my mom. The reality hits me like a bullet to the chest. For everything I'll ever need her for—picking out a wedding dress, parenting advice, a shoulder to cry on—she won't be there. The sudden rush of grief is all-encompassing, and it snatches the air right from my lungs. It's such a waste of life. It's not fair. Why does Dad get to have a happily ever after, and Mom gets nothing at all?

My life will never be the same again. I'll never get to come back to Canada, never get to see Cara again, never get to call myself by my own given name again. I used to wish I could start life over in a new place with a new identity, and now it's actually happening. The old Alyssa jinxed it, and I want to grab her and shake her, tell her *you don't want this, trust me. You don't realize what you'll be throwing away. APPRECIATE EVERYONE IN YOUR LIFE, PLEASE.*

"Don't cry, guys," Pete says softly, and I open my eyes, swiping the tears away. I didn't even notice I'd been crying.

"Well, you're about to kill my fucking mother, so I have every right to cry!" Harper shrieks.

"Hey, don't swear. You're way too young for that."

"I don't give a shit!"

"Well, actually, I do have something to confess, and I don't want you to be mad at me. But I'm not actually going to kill your mother. As much as I want to, I think she needs to be kept alive to suffer. I came here for someone else, actually." Pete pivots and raises the gun to Dad's temple. "Dan, why don't you take a seat."

The whole room falls deafeningly silent. Relief floods Mom's features, and Dad's face turns a ghostly white as he slowly raises his hands in the air. "Whoa, what? Pete? What are you…? Put that down."

"I came here to take back what's mine. Levi is my son. And you stole him from me."

CHAPTER 27

The ground rips from beneath my feet. I couldn't have heard that right. Levi is *Pete's* son?

The energy in the room has shifted, like the air has been completely drained from it. My head swims. I pull Levi tighter to my chest, my brain a jumbled mess of confusion, theories, scenes replaying. Pete isn't going to waltz in here and take my little brother from me, not even out of my cold, dead hands.

Pete's hand tightens around the gun. "You *knew* it this whole time, Dan. And so did you, Melissa. Both of you never gave me the chance to see my son."

Mom blanches, and Dad covers his face with his hands. Both are rendered completely silent. It's all the confirmation I need that Pete is telling the truth. The knife of it slices through my heart, tearing it open with tremendous force. We haven't only lived a lie online these last seven years; it's continued behind the camera, too.

Levi trembles in my arms, clutching me tighter. "You're not my dad," he tells Pete.

"Is that so? Well, the good news is that you know who your real mom is; she's sitting right in front of me. It'll take some time for you to come around to it, but *I'm* your real dad." Pete points to his own chest. "Me. Not that excuse of a man next to you."

Dad starts to sputter out a protest, but Pete holds a hand up to silence him. "Did you think I would honestly help you kidnap your own kids just because you're my friend? It's never that simple, Dan. You raised my kid for seven whole years and thought I'd never find out."

My heart pounds in my ears. "Mom, you—?"

"Yep, she cheated." Pete smirks. "Maybe that makes me a bad person, too, knowing we were both married. Especially considering her husband was my friend. But we all make mistakes, right? We were both going through rough patches in our marriages, and it was like an escape from it all. Wouldn't you say that, Mel? You said Dan was treating you like garbage, didn't you?"

Mom swallows, her face reddening. "Well, yes, but—"

"No buts. I want you to explain it one more time, this time to your kids. I think they deserve to know a little more about your secret life that I know you were never planning to tell them."

Mom takes a deep, shuddering breath. I silently plead with her to tell me Pete is making it up, that there's some other explanation for why he's here, but she breaks me all over again when the words tumble from her mouth in a rush. "Yes, it's true," she says, her voice barely above a whisper. "I'm not trying to place blame on anyone, or justify it in any way, but I'll explain so you can understand what my thought process was at the time. Your dad was starting to give me a hard time about the channel, and I didn't want to give up the career I was so passionate about. He was distant, angry, constantly staying late at work, and overall treating me terribly. I didn't know how to handle it. Then Pete and I met at a work party and got to talking, and suddenly there was someone who actually listened to what I had to say. It's not right, I know. But it went on for three months.

"As soon as I got that positive pregnancy test, I knew. I confessed to your dad right away, and he obviously wasn't happy. Our initial plan was that we were going to divorce, but in the end, we decided to work through our issues together and continue to raise our family. I hate admitting this out loud, but we felt we were much better off financially to raise Levi than Pete was, so we didn't say anything."

Pete laughs bitterly. "I found out a couple years ago, when I saw him for the first time. All of you with brown hair, except for little blond Levi. Not to mention, he looks exactly like me."

Horror drapes over me like a weighted blanket as I stare into Pete's features and realize he's right. The same eyes, same chin, same high cheekbones. A connection I never would've made before today, considering this is my first time meeting Pete. I never thought twice about Levi being the only one in our family having blond hair; it happens in families sometimes, right? Genetics can do some pretty crazy things.

It's not the first time we've been stabbed in the back since we were kidnapped; the wound has been reopened countless times with each new truth revealed, to the point where I'm expecting it to happen again. What else could they be keeping from us? What other ways will my world be completely turned upside down in the coming days, weeks, months? How will I ever trust either of my parents ever again?

I can't. But I'll be eighteen next year, and with any luck, I'll be able to take Harper and Levi somewhere far away from Sawyer and never have to see Mom or Dad again. Cara can come with us, and we can live out our dreams in a big city like Los Angeles or New York. The opportunities are endless.

Levi squirms, burying his face into the crook of my arm, and I'm transported back to the day my ten-year-old self held my baby brother for the first time. As I stared at his tiny, sleeping face, I dreamed of everything I'd teach him one day; how to walk, how to ride a bike, how to skate, how to ace a game of Uno. I knew I'd be his biggest protector forever; if anyone wanted to mess with him, they'd have to deal with his crazy big sister first. I know that's one thing that'll never change. As I look at him now, I know I have a duty to protect him, to keep Pete as far away from him as possible.

I look at Pete now, and a hot rage bubbles deep inside me. He doesn't get to show up here with a gun and start making demands like this. I have to stop him somehow.

Pete paces the room again, the floor creaking slightly beneath his feet. "So, you can imagine what a slap in the face it was to me when Dan approached me at work one day to vent, and ended up confessing to regretting his kids. Not only does he have *my* kid, but he says he regrets him. That could've been a perfect opportunity for him to confess that Levi is mine, that I could take care of him, but nope.

"Dan, you also knew that my wife and I struggled with infertility, and I thought your confession was extremely insensitive. She knows about Levi and what I did, and it's a part of our marriage we're still working to fix. But we've been trying so hard to have a family, and here you are, wishing you didn't have yours. You have everything we've ever wanted. And I think I'm going to take it from you."

Dad pulls himself to his feet. "Don't you dare. You're insane if you think you're just going to take my kids away."

"Why is that insane? You don't want them. Both of you don't even deserve them. I'd like to think they're much better off with my wife and I, even if we don't make as much money as you do."

"No way we're going with you," I tell him through gritted teeth. "You can't make us."

"Oh, yes I can. And I will."

"I'll be better," Mom pleads. "You can't do this. You can't tell me I don't want my kids when I clearly do. And you're going to traumatize them more than they already are."

"It's going to take them some time to adjust, but they'll quickly learn that their lives can be so much better away from the online world, and away from parents who don't appreciate them enough."

"So your plan has been to kidnap my kids from Dan after *he* kidnapped them? I don't...this doesn't make any sense to me."

"Well, when Dan first brought up the idea of planning to take his kids, it planted that seed in my head that maybe this would be a good opportunity for me. All I had to do was pretend to want to help him, then later, take them for myself. Then your video went up, and he wanted to do it *now*. None of my cottages were rented, so it worked out perfectly. I was going to give them a few more days to spend with their dad, but then they escaped, so of course I had to act quickly."

"You make me sick," she spits.

Pete shrugs. "You dug your own grave, Mel. Do you even understand how badly it hurt to watch you get to live this luxurious lifestyle after everything you did? Getting to be rich and famous from all the content you made about the kid you took from me? Maybe you got pregnant on purpose. We all know how many video topics you can make with a new baby. Announcing you're pregnant, telling your friends and family, 'bumpdates,' gender reveal, name reveal...the list goes on."

"Enough. I didn't have a baby for content. No one does that. And if we're going to start playing the blame game, Dan is just as guilty."

I roll my eyes. It's just like Mom to throw Dad under the bus.

"Oh I know. Duh. That's why I'm here in the first place."

If I keep him talking, it could buy us time. The mangled BMW is still parked on the side of the road, and with any luck, someone will have seen it and called the police, even if they didn't recognize it as Dad's. There's still pieces of twisted metal scattered on the road; surely, someone will want to report the accident. There's not much traffic on this road, and it's early in the morning, but I can't lose hope yet. "If you're planning to leave the country with us, people will notice you and your wife suddenly disappeared," I say. "And if you're planning to keep my parents alive, they're obviously going to tell the police what you did."

"The police aren't going to find us," he says confidently. "I have some real estate investor connections in other countries who can get us suitable accommodations. They'd never tell a soul."

"Where are you taking us? I don't want it to be kept a secret. I want to know now."

"I'd love to tell you, sweetheart. But I can't in front of your parents. I don't want them putting a target on our backs."

"And how, exactly, will you manage to leave the country with us? There's an active Amber Alert."

"Don't you go worrying about that. I have it all figured out. And, obviously, your parents are still in the room, so I can't say anything."

"But what about—?"

"Shh."

His sudden sharp tone takes me by surprise. His gaze darts frantically around the room, the colour draining from his face. A twinge of annoyance starts in my core. "What? What are you—?"

He shushes me again, pressing a finger to his lips. He must hear something. The room falls eerily silent, minus the gentle hum of the refrigerator. I strain my ears to listen, watching as his eyebrows knit together in confusion.

Then I hear it.

Sirens. Very distant, but unmistakable.

Our ticket to freedom.

"They're coming from the highway," Pete announces. "Shit. We've gotta go."

Then, everything seems to happen in slow motion. Pete lunges for me, clamping his hand tightly around my arm and yanking me to my feet. Levi topples onto the floor with a thud. Dad yells out for Pete to stop, and just as he springs up from the couch, Pete fires a single shot in Dad's direction. The blast is louder than anything I've heard before, and I hit the floor, cupping my ears. Harper screams, but I don't hear it over the overwhelming ringing sound.

Dad folds over, his face twisting into a look of agony as he holds his left leg. Blood spurts out between his fingertips, and horror snakes its way through me as the realization dawns on me; Pete shot my father. He actually did it. And if we don't follow him out the door, he might do the same to us.

I don't want to look, but I can't peel my eyes away from the gruesome scene. It's self torture. I don't stop until Pete blocks my view, bending in front of me. He grabs a fistful of my hair, and I yelp as he pulls me backwards, sending blinding pain shooting through my scalp. Once I'm on my feet again, he trains the gun on my siblings and I, pointing to the side door. "Outside, now," he barks. I feel the cool metal of the gun press into my spine. "I don't want to have to hurt you."

My hearing makes its way back to me as I rush out of the house, listening for the quickly-approaching sirens. I don't even get to say goodbye to Mom, and I choke on a sob as he leads us to the beat-up Corolla I smashed almost an hour ago. I might be mad at her right now, but I'll never be able to live without her. *Please officers, hurry up. Don't let him take us. I want my mom.*

With a heavy heart, I rip open the passenger door and slide inside.

CHAPTER 28
LAST YEAR

When I get home from school, it's immediately apparent that something isn't right.

There's a stillness to the house, almost as if no one's home, but both my parents' cars are in the driveway. Dad is supposed to be at work. Panic stirs in the pit of my stomach. Did Grandma die? Did someone get hurt? Am I in trouble for something?

The *thump* of my backpack hitting the floor is like a door slamming in the quiet space. I involuntarily flinch. "Mom? Dad?"

Nothing. My heart jackhammers in my chest as I slowly make my way to the living room, finding it empty. The TV is off. Mom isn't in her usual spot on the couch, laptop cradled in her lap, editing a vlog. This isn't good. "Hello? Mom?"

"In here," comes Dad's voice, all the way from the kitchen. His tone is softer than usual, which only adds to my growing concern. I could convince myself he's home early because he had a dentist appointment, or it was a slower day at the office, but I can count on one hand the number of times he's been home early in my entire sixteen years of life.

I head toward the kitchen, sweat gathering in my armpits. Mom and Dad are seated at the dining room table, hands folded in front of them. Mom's eyes are red and swollen, like she's been crying. I feel faint. "What happened?" I blurt. Someone must be dead.

Dad blows out a breath and gestures to the chair across from him. "Sit, please. We need to tell you something."

"Is Grandma okay?"

Dad furrows his brow. "Of course she is," he says as I drop down into the chair, like it's the most obvious thing in the world.

"Okay. What did you need to tell me?"

"We were going to wait until Harper and Levi got home so we could tell you all together, but that's half an hour from now and you're probably wondering why I'm home early. So, we might as well cut to the chase and say it now. Your mom and I have been thinking about it for a long time, but…we're getting a divorce."

The confession hangs in the air for a moment. It's funny; I always thought this type of news would devastate me, but I feel nothing. It should land like a bomb into my world, blowing my seemingly-perfect life to pieces, but all is calm. I saw this coming from a million miles away. It takes every ounce of strength in me not to shrug and say, "Okay." That'd be kind of a dick move.

Instead, I let my face fall a little. "Really?"

Mom nods solemnly. "Yes, and we don't mean to hurt you by telling you this. We've been unhappy for a while; I'm sure you know that. It's not your fault in any way. It's just between your father and I."

"We've been fighting a lot, and I know it's not good for you three to constantly have to hear it," Dad adds. "It's not fair to you that we aren't getting along. We've decided, going forward, that we'd much rather have two happy households than one unhappy one."

"Exactly. Your dad will be moving out, and he's already found the perfect place in Toronto that you guys are going to love. We'll work out a custody schedule, but we want to make it fair for you."

"I know you have questions." Dad covers my hand with his. "We're happy to answer any of them. This is a really tough conversation to have, and we know it's probably hard for you to hear. We're here for you no matter what."

I lean back against the chair, numb. I can't believe this is finally happening. What they're saying is a massive understatement—they've been much more than simply *unhappy* for forever—but it's a relief to know it's finally over. For a little while, anyway. "What's happening with the channel?" I ask.

Mom perks up, as if she's been waiting for this question. Isn't it sad how it's the first one that came to mind? "Nothing is really changing, aside from your dad no longer being on it. He hasn't been on it in a while, anyway, but the content itself will remain the same."

Dad sighs heavily. "Obviously, I'm against it. I just don't think—"

"*Dan*. We're not having this discussion in front of Alyssa. She's heard enough of this over the last year or so. This is between you and I from now on."

"Sure. Fine."

"How often do we see you?" I meet eyes with Dad. "It can't be evenly split custody if you're living in Toronto. That's, like, forty minutes away. Getting to and from school would suck."

"I know." He shakes his head, and the wrinkles in his forehead deepen. "There wasn't much on the rental market in Sawyer, so I had no choice but to move closer to work instead. We're thinking I'll see you on weekends, at least. If not every weekend, then every other weekend."

"I know it's not as often as you're used to," says Mom. "It's going to be an adjustment for sure, so if you or your brother and sister need to talk to us, we're always here to listen. That will never change."

"Okay." The situation is less than ideal, but at least we won't be living out of a backpack.

"Do you have any other questions? Anything that's worrying you?"

I shake my head. "Nope." It's the truth; I've been waiting for this day to come for a while now, so I can't find it in me to feel stressed or anxious about it. Their jabs during the day and harsh whispers during the night have become as much of a daily routine in this household as brushing my teeth or changing clothes.

I think back to that night in the Santa Fe hotel last month, when I overheard Mom tell Dad she wanted a divorce. There was bitter silence in the car for the rest of the trip, but when we returned home, there was no mention of it again; at least, not while I was within earshot. It looks like they've finally settled on a decision instead of dancing around the subject for months. A sense of hope floods me. Despite still having to be on the channel, the atmosphere in this house is going to feel a lot more positive, not like the warzone it's been. No more walking on eggshells, terrified to piss someone off. As long as I'm not still caught up in their drama, I'm happy to let them do what I've been secretly begging them to do all along.

I know, without a doubt, the channel is the biggest reason behind their divorce. It's Mom's pride and joy, and it's Dad's worst nightmare. But after fighting so hard for change, he's just…giving up on us. Leaving us to deal with the problem. I bite my tongue, wishing I could accuse him right to his face, but he'll only get defensive and claim it's not his fault.

Okay, so maybe I lied; there's *one* thing that bothers me about their divorce, and it's that Dad chose to walk away instead of try harder to make a change for us. But they can't know that. So, I simply go up to my room, shut the door, and pick a thriller from my nightstand while they repeat the conversation to Harper and Levi downstairs.

CHAPTER 29
NOW

Pete throws the Corolla in reverse before I've buckled my seatbelt, and I flop against the back of the seat like a ragdoll. "Move your head," he growls as he approaches the end of the driveway. "I can't see."

I swear under my breath and duck out of his way. My seatbelt clicks into place, and behind me, I hear Harper and Levi do the same. "Please don't do this," Harper begs through her tears. "Please. I'm scared."

"Shut up," Pete barks. He reaches the end of the driveway, and that's when two police cars come barreling around the corner from the direction of the highway, red and blue lights flashing angrily. A flicker of relief snakes its way through me, but it's snatched away just as quickly when Pete guns the engine and steers the car in the opposite direction, toward the cottage we just came from. My hand instinctively flies to the grab handle above the door. Harper and Levi scream, and I clamp my mouth shut to avoid doing the same.

Pete releases a string of curse words as he tears down the road, accelerating faster and faster with each passing second. I've never gone this fast in a vehicle before, and panic stirs in my stomach as graphic images of car accidents dance in my head. How am I supposed to trust Pete isn't going to kill us? I'm going to go on a whim and assume Pete has never driven a racecar before, especially not on a winding dirt road like this one. The police are hot on our heels, but how are they going to stop him without causing an accident?

We might die today. It's a cold, hard fact that hits me like a swift punch to the gut, and I hug myself, as if to shield myself from the blow. I'm not ready. My life has barely started, and there's so much more I want to do. So many more places I want to see. So many goals I want to accomplish. I might never get to, all because of Dad's decisions, Mom's decisions, Pete's decisions.

Everyone in our lives has failed us.

Pete splashes into a pothole, and the car swerves slightly. I brace for impact, my heart in my throat, but the car corrects itself and continues straight ahead. The sirens wail behind us, and a glance in my mirror shows they're catching up quick. One of the cruisers moves to drive beside us, but Pete punches the accelerator again, sending chunks of mud flying through the air. The cruisers do the same.

My jaw tenses. I hope this road eventually leads back to the highway; that would mean more cops will approach from that direction to stop us. Maybe they'll throw down some spike strips like they do in the movies. If that's true, we're still going to crash. Either way—whether we're stopped or not—this won't end favourably.

The trees sail past us at an unbelievable speed. I catch sight of the other cottage for a brief second, and in the blink of an eye, it's gone, replaced with more views of the forest. A part of me prefers to be back there in the basement, plotting a different escape rather than being trapped in the car that's hurtling us toward a new life. Would we have made it out safely, had I come up with a better plan? Maybe not, but I did everything I could, which has to count for something.

I imagine reaching across the centre console and yanking the steering wheel from Pete's hands. If we weren't going so fast, I'd consider actually doing it, but at this rate, we're going to wrap ourselves around a tree. He still has the gun tucked into his waistband, but it's too far for me to reach. There has to be *something* I can do to help the cops stop him. I've been flying by the seat of my pants all night, but even now, I come up empty; every idea I have seems to point to instant death.

Pete brakes for a sharp corner up ahead, and for one terrifying moment, the car fishtails, the force throwing my head against the passenger window. Pain explodes through my skull, and my breath hitches in my throat. *It's over. It's over.* More screams erupt from the backseat, and beside me, Pete's hands scramble against the wheel, fighting for control of the car. We drift around the corner, skidding into the grass, and then suddenly we're back on track, racing down a straight stretch of road. My thighs burn with relief.

"Slow the hell down, Pete," I hear myself say. My head pounds. "You're going to kill us."

"I can't slow down!" he yells. "Do you honestly think that would help us? Do you not see the cops behind us?"

"Well, it's your fault you got us in this situation. You deserve to get caught."

"Shut up, Alyssa. I'm trying to concentrate."

More cottages appear to our right, and when my gaze lands on them, a lump lodges itself in my throat, choking the sob that rises within me. I can't help but mentally kick myself for choosing to run the opposite way when we escaped. This way would've been much quicker, and there are even cars in the driveways. I know for a fact these people would've helped us. Dad wouldn't have expected us to go this way, and it would've thrown off both Dad and Pete's plans. We wouldn't be in this car right now. An anchor of guilt sinks into my stomach. It's not just my parents and Pete who have failed us; I have, too.

Oh, for fuck's sake, Alyssa, stop feeling bad for yourself. It's not going to change anything.

But I can't stop. This is partially my fault, and I know I need to calm down in order to think rationally, but I don't know how. Not with the fear of the unknown closing around me like a fist.

One of the officers approaches the left side of the Corolla again, closing in on us to attempt a PIT maneuver, but Pete swerves away into the front lawn of one of the cottages, striking the mailbox in the corner of the driveway. The seatbelt digs into my shoulder blade and my waist as I'm propelled forward, and I clench my teeth. "Hang on tight," Pete tells us as he steers back toward the road.

Once again, Pete narrowly avoids being sideswiped as the tires connect with the dirt. *Come on guys, stop him!* Desperation to escape the car claws at me. The police can't just let someone like Pete outsmart them; surely, this isn't their first high speed chase. It's like a violent video game come to life, only I'm the character who has no control over my own fate. It's in the hands of the good characters or the bad characters; whichever one wins.

It's too bad I didn't hit the front of the Corolla instead of the rear passenger door. Maybe I could've wrecked the engine. I, unfortunately, seem to have hit the perfect spot, considering the tires are also in perfect condition. I can't say the same for the BMW, and I don't imagine Dad's worried about the damage done to his prized car anymore.

My heart wrenches. Despite the complicated feelings I have toward him, I hope he's alive and the paramedics made it to him on time. The moment he was shot replays in my head like the remnants of a nightmare; blood spatter coating the white floor, his anguished cries muffled by the echoes of the gunshot, the betrayal etched into his features. If he lives, he may never walk properly again. Just like mine, his life will never be the same after today, but I won't lie and say he doesn't deserve it. Whatever happens to my siblings and I today will be his fault, just as much as it's Pete's.

"Dammit," Pete hisses suddenly, glancing in the rearview mirror. "There's more of them."

I sneak a peek behind us, and sure enough, three more cops have shown up. In the backseat, Harper clutches Levi's hand tightly as she follows my gaze. "Oh my God," she whimpers. "Pete, please. You have to give up."

"She's right." My voice shakes. "Look what you're doing. This isn't better than what my parents put us through, right? If you cared, you wouldn't put us in danger like this."

"We're going to be fine," he says coldly. "I was going to slam on the brakes and turn around. We can't now, obviously, but there's got to be a better plan. We just need to keep going."

"You don't have a plan. There's no way this will work."

"I didn't ask for your opinion, Alyssa."

"But seriously. How well do you know this road? Have you ever evaded police before? And where's your wife in all this?"

"Let me concentrate," he snaps. "I can't with you mouthing off next to me."

"I just want to know why you'd—"

Pete gasps, and I snap my head up to see the lining of trees directly ahead of us, the road curving in front of it. A dead end. To the right, a clearing leading to the lake. Pete slams on the brakes, but before I know it we're fishtailing again, and we have nowhere to go. We swerve left, then right, then left, then right. The next few seconds happen so quickly I don't have time to brace myself for the incoming disaster.

Harper and Levi's combined screams are drowned out by the sound of my pulse pounding in my ears. We're sliding, sliding, spinning, until we're finally thrown over the edge, and the Corolla plunges nose-first into the lake.

CHAPTER 30

I don't remember my neck snapping forward on impact. I don't remember the feel of the world tilting on its axis. I don't remember the punch of the seatbelt against my body. What I do remember, however, is that my siblings are in the backseat, and I need to make sure they're okay.

Water quickly begins to rise around us as we sink, and I kick into action. I click the seatbelt off and launch myself toward the backseat where, much to my relief, Harper and Levi are also alive. "Get your seatbelts off," I bark. "We need to get out of here *now*."

They do as told without hesitating. "I don't wanna die," Levi hiccups as he watches the water outside the window.

"We don't have time to whine about dying, Levi," says Harper. "We have to get out of here before we *do* die!"

I hoist myself up by the tops of the front seats, and any attempt at crawling back there with them is suddenly stopped by Pete, whose hand clamps down on my shoulder. "You're not going anywhere, you little bitch," he hisses. His other fist goes into my hair again, and I yelp as he drags me back to the front seat.

The car begins to tilt to the right. "Open the window!" I yell to my siblings. "Open Levi's window, behind Pete. Do it now before we're completely submerged."

I jab my elbow into Pete's nose with a sickening *crack*, and he cries out, though he doesn't loosen his grip on me. Panic rises within me like the water surrounding us, threatening to drown me. I notice he hasn't unbuckled his seatbelt yet, and a cold grip of panic seizes me when I realize why; a captain always goes down with his ship. He has no intention of leaving this car, and he's going to take me down with him.

163

Why, I can't seem to figure out. Is it because I'm fighting back? Is it because I called him out on his lack of a plan? Am I somehow a threat to him?

I don't have time to think it over. That can come later, when my nightmares chase any chance of sleep away. Right now, I need to focus solely on surviving.

"It's not opening!" Harper cries, her voice bordering on hysteria. "Oh my God. What do we do? *What do we do?*"

She takes notice of Pete's hands on me, and her features pinch together in a scowl. "Get your hands off my sister, you freak! What is wrong with you?" She begins slapping his arm, but he doesn't react. "Let her go! You're not taking her with you."

"Harper, *get out*. Don't wait for me. Go to the other side of the car while you have time."

"I'm not leaving you—"

"Open the window, climb out, and help Levi out after you."

She hesitates for a second, then reaches to her left and successfully rolls down her window. Pete gives another tug on my hair as I try to follow, and ripples of pain travel through my scalp, followed by the warm trickle of blood. His other arm reaches around my neck in a headlock, and he pulls me toward the steering wheel. "You don't listen, do you?" he says with gritted teeth. "Are you always this difficult to deal with?"

He squeezes tighter, cutting off even more of my air supply. My eyes bulge from the pressure. "Why do you want me to die with you?" I manage.

"Because, no matter what, you think your mom's always right. You're just going to repeat the cycle with your kids. Have as many of them as possible so you can exploit—"

"Don't you dare." I gasp for air, the corners of my vision turning black. "I'm not like her. You don't know me."

"You're on her side. You always will be. And the world doesn't need any more people like that."

I watch as Harper climbs through the window and, once she's in the water, she reaches for Levi's hand and pulls him out with her, sobbing. They're safe outside the car, where the police are waiting, and that's all that matters. Meanwhile, Pete and I are sinking quicker and quicker, and the clock is ticking. It's a matter of minutes before death takes me in its embrace, and any chance I had at making things right with my family will be gone.

Stars swim in my vision. Slowly but surely, my flailing arms lose their strength, and I collapse against him, exhausted. I could wait for the police to get to us, but by then, it'll be too late. Tears well in my eyes at the thought. I hate Pete. I hate him so freaking much for robbing me of a future, for pretending to care about me, for hurting my entire family. My death is going to kill Mom, and Harper and Levi will always remember the last time they saw me; being strangled by Pete. They're going to carry that grief with them for the rest of their lives, wishing they could have done something, even though it's not their fault.

The car bobs up and down, and some of the water begins to pour in through the open window. I've always wondered what it would be like to drown, to spend your last moments thrashing underwater, gasping for air. I heard somewhere that it's supposed to be the most peaceful way to die. I don't see how being fully awake and unable to breathe could be peaceful, but maybe there's supposed to be some kind of calm feeling wash over me with the waves. I'll find out any minute.

"You still awake, there, *Lissy*?" Pete says, his tone mocking.

Water splashes against my bare legs, and my hands instinctively fly to them, the cold sending shockwaves through my body. My hand brushes against the pocket of my shorts, and that's when I feel the hard lump tucked inside, pressing against my thigh. Confusion overtakes me for a second, but then I remember my last-minute decision back in the basement, and suddenly there's light at the end of the tunnel.

"I don't want to die," I tell him as I slowly reach into my pocket to extract the glass shard I wrapped up hours ago. I won't, now.

"Shh. It'll be over any minute now." He strokes my cheek with one hand, slightly loosening his grip around my neck. "I don't want to die, either. My wife will be so confused when I don't show up. But life isn't always fair."

"No, it's not." I unwrap the shard slowly, without looking down. Thankfully, Pete doesn't notice. The water licks at my ankles more fiercely now, rising higher with each passing second, and I know I don't have much time left. "I'm too young to die. I wish I told my family I loved them more often."

"Well, unfortunately, you can't undo the past. There's no use spending your last moments thinking about all your regrets. Just try and remember the good times."

My heart races. I think I'm going to be sick, but I swallow the nausea and clear my throat as I position the shard between my fingers. *You can do this. You have to. There's no other way out of here.*

"I'm sorry it had to end like this," says Pete. "I didn't mean for any of us to die."

"And I'm *not* sorry for what I have to do to survive." I suck in a deep breath, and with all the strength I have left in me, I drive the shard right into his neck.

NEW VIDEO FROM THEBENNETTFAM
NEW BEGINNINGS

Hey, everyone. I know it's been a while since I've shown my face on this channel, and I'm sure you all understand why. The last month has been an absolute rollercoaster for my family and I, so the break from posting has been amazing. I debated whether or not to make this video, but in the end, I decided I have to start putting my family first, and it feels as though I haven't been doing that for a long time. It sounds horrible, and it is.

So, effective immediately, I will be leaving YouTube. Not forever, but whenever I do *decide to post, things are going to work a little differently. Alyssa, Harper and Levi will no longer be in any of my videos, and instead my videos will be just about me and the things I love. I also won't be daily vlogging anymore, or have a set schedule for when I post. You might get a video once a month, or once a year; it all depends on how I'm feeling.*

If there's one thing I learned from this whole situation, I should never have forced my passion onto my kids like this, and made their whole lives public for anyone around the world to see. Because my kids are obviously such a huge part of my life, I initially saw nothing wrong with what I was doing. But this channel became an obsession, and suddenly I found myself willing to do anything for content, even if it made my kids uncomfortable. I'll never forgive myself for that, and this is not me asking you to feel bad for me in any way. I knew what I was doing, and it's about time I started holding myself accountable for the harm I've been putting my children through.

It should have been no one's business that my daughters started their periods, or that my kids were struggling with potty training, or that they had a crush at school. I think back to all of my own embarrassing moments from my childhood and cringe at the thought of having it publicized for strangers to pick apart. But while filming these moments, I thought I was helping other parents who may have been experiencing the same things. I realize, now, that it's not my responsibility to make other parents feel less alone, much less take away my kids' privacy to accomplish that. It sounds harsh, but it's the reality.

In some ways, social media can be a great thing, too. For one, the kidnapping brought so many people together around the world to help look for my children, and word spread like wildfire that they were missing. I'll be forever grateful for that. This job has allowed me to connect with so many wonderful people, and I'm so thankful there are people out there who genuinely care about my family and I, even if they've never met us. I wouldn't trade it for the world. For those of you that have supported me throughout my journey, I appreciate you more than you'll ever know.

However, social media can also be an extremely toxic place. There's such a heavy pressure to be perfect, and for a while, I thought my content was "different" because I'd post how "unperfect" my family could be, like my young kids throwing tantrums. I thought I was being authentic. But not only that; I also lived for social media content. We'd travel to certain places just so I could make a vlog out of it, and post pretty pictures to Instagram. I never lived in the moment. Even when the kids needed me most—like when they were sick or injured—I took it as a content opportunity, recording them at their most vulnerable. And, I'll be completely honest, there were plenty of times I lied for views, which is just...disgusting.

It's what led Dan to kidnap the kids.

Well, it was more the straw that broke the camel's back. Alyssa came to me just before the kidnapping to say she was tired of faking things for the camera, so I stupidly decided, what better way to deal with this than film a story time about the divorce? And I lied. Yes, our marriage was terrible toward the end, which is why we divorced, but Dan never drained our bank account. He didn't do half the things I accused him of. And why did I accuse him of these things? To increase our views and engagement. What does increased views lead to? More money.

It's sick.

Throughout the years, I constantly found myself lying about things for this exact reason, and if I wasn't outright lying, I was making clickbait titles to capture interest. It was an easy strategy to get views. The channel's numbers skyrocketed, and to be totally honest, so did our bank account, so I thought this made me successful. I lost sight of *the real reason I started this channel, which was to make meaningful connections with other moms around the world. My addiction spiraled out of control to the point that, looking back, I hardly recognize myself. Since when did I start caring so much about keeping up a fake persona? Why did other people's opinions of my family, whether good or bad, matter to me so much? What exactly was I trying to prove?*

I guess I was trying to prove that just because you're a teen parent, it doesn't make you a bad *parent. Dan and I didn't plan to be teen parents, and we'd never encourage anyone to do it, but we made the most out of our situation. What* does *make you a bad parent, though, is treating your kids as though they don't come first, and I basically ended up becoming a bad parent while trying to prove to the world that I'm a good parent.*

God, I'm rambling. But you get what I mean, right?

So, it's about time to do what I should've done a long time ago, and make spending time with my family my top priority. I can make memories with my kids without shoving a camera into their faces. No one needs to know what we're having for breakfast, or where we're travelling to next, or where we got our outfits from. I'm finally going to give us all the privacy we need, and while it's not going to fix everything that's broken, it's a start.

My kids aren't just props I can use for viral videos; they're human beings with real feelings. They make mistakes sometimes, just like I do, and just like everyone else in this world does. I need to stop holding them to these impossible standards because people on the internet said so. It will forever be my biggest regret, so going forward, I need to step away from this channel, because of how unhealthy it's become in all our lives.

Like I said earlier, I'm so grateful for all of you that have supported me, and I know you'll understand why I need to do this. I'm really excited to see what this next chapter holds for my family, off camera and fully present. Thanks for watching, and see you later.

CHAPTER 31

FOUR MONTHS LATER

"You're not seriously enjoying that, are you?" Cara curls her lip dramatically at the book I've just set down next to me on our lunch table; a cheesy young adult slasher that's exploded in popularity on TikTok recently.

I grin. "The concept is a little stupid, I know. But it's honestly kind of fun."

"There's no way you just said that." She gags. "It's, like, one of the worst books I've ever read. A literal steaming pile of garbage."

"But it's subjective."

"Whatever you need to say to justify that horrible purchase," she says, and I laugh.

I've missed our banter. Ever since I returned home four months ago, everyone has walked on eggshells around me, terrified that they'll say the wrong thing and I'll break. Even Cara, who's always making fun of me for something. No one knows how to talk to me—whose name went from The Girl From YouTube to The Girl Who Was Kidnapped—and all I want is to go back to how things were before. I'm not fragile. There's nothing anyone at school can say that could possibly be worse than what I went through.

Is it bad that I'd almost *prefer* to be bullied rather than having my ass kissed?

Cara is finally coming around to the fact I won't burst into tears if she criticizes me for something as unimportant as book preferences. I'll take it. She's never been one to hold back, and I've always loved that about her. Perhaps I act too relaxed about what happened to me in the public eye, but the last thing I need is more attention. Truth be told, I'd rather forget about it and find a way to move forward.

It's not easy, though, when that warm July morning regularly plagues my nightmares.

"Hey, just because it's popular doesn't always mean it's bad." I wave the book in front of her and take a bite of my sandwich. "It's supposed to be a little ridiculous. That's what makes it entertaining."

"But it's so cliché. Have we not learned that the dumb-girl-versus-killer trope is overdone? That Geneveive chick had so many opportunities to escape, and then she left the knife right next to the killer. Seriously. No one could possibly be this stupid in real life."

"I know. But maybe the pressure got to her or something, and she panicked."

"You never did anything like that." She winks. "You were *such* a badass when you escaped. Plus, you kept Harper and Levi safe, too. You're, like, a hero."

"*Ookay.*" I lean back and raise my palms in front of me. I'll never get used to getting called that. To me, I was doing what anyone else would do in that situation; put the younger kids first. "It really wasn't anything special. I just—"

"Alyssa, you really need to give yourself more credit." Her tone takes on a serious note, and she lets her smile drop. "You killed a man to survive. You took a million risks over the course of a few days, but especially the night you escaped. It's because of *you* that you and your siblings aren't still stuck in that basement, wondering when you'll get out. Instead of waiting, you took action and made it happen. So, please, don't try and convince me you barely had a role in it, when you did something that most of us wouldn't be brave enough to do."

Unexpectedly, tears spring to my eyes, and I wipe them away with the back of my hand. *Brave* is never a word I thought would be used to describe me; most of the time, it's *spoiled rich girl* or *nerd* or *awkward*. It's quite simply the greatest compliment I've received, but at the same time, I don't know how I'll ever get over the guilt of killing Pete, even if he deserved it. I had no choice but to be brave, otherwise I'd have died alongside him in the water.

Spurting blood. Gushing ice cold water. Screaming. Gasping for air. The vacant stare of someone who's no longer alive.

I shudder.

"Hey, I hope I didn't upset you." Cara's soft voice filters in through the noise in my head, and she snakes her arm around my shoulders. "You've just been really hard on yourself. I know you don't want to make a big deal about what happened, but you should be kinder to yourself. You're like the strong, independent women we've been reading about. Totally unlike the girl in that dumpster fire you're reading right now."

That gets a chuckle out of me. "Well, thank you. Really. I'm trying to get past it all, but I still end up thinking about it every day." I sniffle. God, I'm crying in the cafeteria. "And I know I'm not the only one. Levi wakes up screaming a lot. So does Harper."

"Shit. That's horrible." Cara shakes her head. "Are you guys still going to therapy?"

"Once a week, yeah."

"Is it helping?"

I shrug. "A little bit, I guess. It probably just needs time."

Almost immediately after Harper, Levi and I were discharged from the hospital later that day in July, Mom insisted we start going to therapy. She told us the last thing she wanted us to do was bottle our feelings up, and that therapy would help us learn healthy ways to navigate the emotions tied to everything we've been through. Including the effects of growing up as public figures. I'll be honest; it's refreshing to see Mom not only admit she was wrong, but to take action. She hasn't filmed another video of us since.

When I need to talk to someone, Mom is always there to listen, without propping up her camera to document it. It's a huge weight lifted off my shoulders, one I thought I'd never get as long as I lived at home. For the first time in my life, I'm experiencing real privacy, and it's a completely foreign feeling. In the entire seventeen years she's been on social media, this marks the first time she's ever truly taken a break. It'll take a long time before I fully trust her, but we're making progress, which is all that matters. She's been in therapy with us, so at least she's willing to make an effort.

"You know what you should do?" Cara tears open the lid of her yogurt and dunks her spoon inside. "You should write a book about what you went through. You read so much; why not try writing?"

A smile takes shape on my face. "I am, actually."

Her jaw drops, and her eyes light right up. "Are you freaking kidding me? That's amazing! I better be the first person to read it."

"You know you will. I only just started it, and I don't know if I'll publish it yet, just for privacy reasons, but for now, it's helping me deal with all the emotional stuff. We'll see. It'd be *so* cool to be an author."

"No shit. It'd be cool to be *best friends* with an author. Oh my God. I'm so happy for you, I could scream."

Warmth fills my chest, and I wrap my arms around her, barely containing my squeal of excitement. "Thank you! I don't know what I'd ever do without you."

"Same to you." When she lets go, her eyes are shining. "I'm so happy you made it out of that cabin alive. I thought I was never going to see you again." She laughs and wipes her eyes. "Dammit, I didn't want to cry today. Thanks a lot."

"Hey, you brought it up first." I join her in the laughter; it's contagious. "You brought it on yourself."

"I can't help it. You're just so…*inspirational.*"

"Oh, come on now."

"You might think I'm just trying to suck up to you. But I mean it. I'm glad you're here."

Now I'm full-on sobbing, and people are starting to stare. Of the millions of compliments I've received in my life, mostly from strangers online, this one means the most. It confirms that every decision I made that day was worth it, and there are people in my personal life who actually care. I don't know what the future holds now, but things can only get better from here. Writing my story is only the next step.

When the bell rings, signaling it's time to head to biology class, my tears have dried, but my chest feels lighter. I'm feeling more inspired than I ever have been, and in the next half hour, I'll be meeting with our school's guidance counsellor to discuss college applications, which I find myself excited for. I used to struggle with the thought of college, and the overwhelming number of options I had, but I think I've narrowed it down to two choices; journalism or criminal justice. After everything I've been through and the way I handled it, they both seemed like suitable options. And, since Dad is no longer in my life, there's no more pressure to attend an Ivy League or pick a career *he* would've wanted for me.

I smirk. He'd hate to hear it.

***

"How was school?" I ask Harper and Levi as they dive into my car, tossing their backpacks at their feet.

"I made a paper mâché pumpkin with my class for Halloween," says Levi. "Ms. Porter said mine looked really good."

"I bet it did. What about you, Harper?"

"It was fine." She frowns as I back out of my parking space and head in the direction of home. "Everyone's still acting so weird around me, though."

I furrow my brows and steer onto the main road. "Weird how?"

"Caleb and Marcus…you know those kids that make fun of me sometimes? Well, they haven't at all this school year. And today, Caleb apologized to me. Then he said he liked me."

If I had a drink in my mouth, I would've spit it out all over the steering wheel. "Like, he has a crush on you?"

"Yeah. Really freaking weird."

I shake my head. "Red flag. A boy should never bully you if he likes you. What did you say to him?"

"I thanked him for saying sorry. Then he asked me out on a date, and I told him to shove his date up his ass."

I holler with laughter. Harper doesn't realize how sassy and fierce she can be sometimes, and I love that about her. At least she knows her worth. "Good for you. Besides, you're way too young to go on a date. At least wait until, like, high school or something."

She curls her lip. "Well, considering I don't like any of the boys in my class, that shouldn't be hard."

A few minutes later, I pull into the driveway and park next to Mom's Mercedes. She's at the door waiting for us, wearing a witch-patterned dress and an ear-to-ear grin. "How was school?" she asks as she pulls us into a group hug. Before we can answer, she says, "I made some Halloween cupcakes for us and got the living room all decorated. I was thinking we could watch a Halloween movie together."

"Ouu, I'd love that," I say. At one point in time, when my parents were still together, we used to do a movie night every Friday and order pizza. It was a tradition we were always consistent with, never missing a single week. Sometimes we were lucky, and Mom would put away the camera for the entire movie. We haven't had a single movie night since Mom and Dad divorced.

With Dad heading to trial soon, I'll admit it does make me a little sad to imagine him stuck in a cold cell, unable to watch movies or have access to any electronics. But at the end of the day, he needs to face the consequences of his actions which, as he told Mom over the phone, he feels he deserves. It's strange; he's been extremely apologetic, constantly stating that everything he'd done had been with good intentions. It's still difficult for me to believe after all the threats he made, but maybe one day I can forgive him. Not any time soon, though.

I still haven't spoken to him over the phone, or even visited him. Giving myself space from him has been best for my mental health, even if a part of me misses him a little. It won't last forever, but for now, it's necessary.

We pile onto the white couch in the living room now, and Mom brings out the plate of cupcakes. "So, which movie are we thinking?" she asks, switching on the TV and dropping down next to us.

"I wanna watch *Monster House*," says Levi.

Harper curls her lip. "I'd rather watch *Coraline*. That one is so much scarier."

"What about *The Shining*?" I half joke, which only earns me glares from my siblings.

"You know that one's not appropriate for kids," says Mom.

"I don't really care which one we watch. Harper and Levi can pick."

In the end, we settle on *Monster House*, and I relax into the couch cushions, feeling the tension release from my shoulders. *Home sweet home.* Four months ago, I thought I'd never be coming back here, and now I make sure to appreciate the small things, like having the opportunity to watch a Halloween movie with my family. It's difficult to imagine where we'd be right now if we hadn't escaped; would we still be locked in that basement, starved of a normal life? Would we be in another country with new identities, plotting another escape? Would we even be alive?

I shudder. I don't want to think about it.

Mom's arm makes its way around my shoulders, pulling me close, and I melt into her. Her other free arm goes around Levi, and Harper manages to squeeze her way in. Mom plants a kiss onto each of our foreheads. "I love you guys so much," she says. "You know that, right?"

"Of course I do," I say, and my siblings nod. "We love you too."

"Let's do this every Friday again. I'll order pizza, and we can pick a movie to watch before we go to bed. Just like old times."

"Yes, that would be awesome."

We stay huddled like that for a long time, even after the movie is over. Harper and Levi are asleep, and Mom strokes their hair, her eyes shining. "I'm so grateful I still get to do this," she whispers to me. "I wouldn't trade this feeling for the world."

"Me too. I still can't believe we got out of there."

Her warm eyes meet mine. "Promise me when you're in college, you'll still see us often?"

"You know I will."

I used to want to get away, but now I want to stay. No matter how old I am, I'll always need my mom. The choices I make now will only strengthen my relationship with her for as many years as I have left with her. I'm going to be fully in control of writing this next chapter of my life, and I know, deep down, that it's about to be the best yet.

ENJOYED THE BOOK? FEEL FREE TO LEAVE A REVIEW!

Reviews matter SO much to authors like me to help spread the word to other fellow readers. If you have a minute, I'd love to hear what you think of *A Familiar Betrayal* on Goodreads or Amazon!

FOLLOW ME ON SOCIAL MEDIA!

Facebook, Instagram, TikTok, YouTube:
@BriannaNorthAuthor

Brianna North is the author of young adult novels *Stay Strong*, *The Other Half of Me*, *Where the Sun Won't Shine*, and *A Familiar Betrayal*. She grew up in a small town in the Sudbury district where she began her writing journey as a child, drawing inspiration from the nature of Northern Ontario. She graduated from the public relations program at Cambrian College and works as a marketing manager. When she's not writing, you'll find her reading a book or playing with her cat, Cooper.

Manufactured by Amazon.ca
Bolton, ON